EYE OF THE

BEHOLDER

& Other Tales

EYE OF THE BEHOLDER

& Other Tales

THE ADVENTURES OF VIOLA STEWART
JOURNAL #2

KAREN J CARLISLE

Kraken Publishing

Eye of the Beholder and Other Tales
The Adventures of Viola Stewart Journal #2

Copyright © 2016 by Karen J Carlisle
Second Edition © 2022 Karen J Carlisle

The moral right of this author has been asserted.

All rights reserved in all media. No part of this book may be reproduced, stored or transmitted in any form, or by any means, without written permission (except under the statutory exceptions of the Australian Copyright Act 1968).

This is a work of fiction. All characters and events in this publication, other than those clearly in public domain, are fictitious. Any resemblance to real persons, living or dead is purely coincidental.

Cover design, photography and artwork, icons and internal artwork:
Copyright © 2022 by Karen J Carlisle
ISBN: 978-0-9944850-7-6

NATIONAL LIBRARY OF AUSTRALIA

A catalogue record for this book is available from the National Library of Australia

Also available separately as eBooks.

This book is written in British English.
Printed in Australia.
First Edition 2016
Second Edition 2022

Typeset in Times Roman 10pt.

Published by Kraken Publishing.
www.krakenpublishing.com

To David, who encouraged me to keep writing,
and my readers who asked for more.

Contents

Three More Short Stories

Novella

Bonus Short Story

Three More Short Stories

A Present for Viola
Point of View
Mars Ascending

A Present for Viola

Children's laughter floated up from the street below the bedroom window. Viola pulled the covers away from her face and rolled onto her back. The sun shone red through her closed eyelid. A cool breeze played over her cheeks; a heady floral scent tickled her nose.

Viola smiled and nestled back under the covers.

She opened her eye. The lace curtains glowed and waltzed in the morning light, licking the edge of the glass vase on the nearby dresser. Rose petals fluttered. Viola drew in a long breath. She loved roses.

Perfect start to the day.

Hooves clopped on the cobblestones below the bedroom window.

Her fingers fumbled on the bedside table. Soft lace tickled her fingertips. She snatched up the eye patch.

A muffled footfall on the front step. A tap on the door below, too quiet to be heard had she still slept.

Viola glanced at the clock. Not quite eight.

Who could it be, at this hour?

She slipped out of bed, padded to the window, and secured the patch's ribbons snugly around her head as she peeked through the slit in the curtains.

A familiar figure emerged from under the portico – tall and lean. Silver waistcoat buttons glinted under his coat, in the morning light.

Henry!

Viola's heart fluttered.

She snatched up her dressing gown from the dresser chair, and slid her arms into the sleeves.

Henry stepped into the waiting carriage. The driver snapped the reins; the carriage rattled off eastwards toward Harley Street.

"Henry?" Viola's voice cracked.

The carriage turned the corner. Henry was gone.

Viola's shoulders slumped. A silken gown sleeve slithered off her shoulder.

Why didn't you stay?

She tugged the sleeve back onto her shoulder and flopped onto the dresser chair.

She stared out the window. The sky was a brilliant blue. Just like Henry's eyes.

Viola twisted the silk gown in her fingers. Why had his leaving bothered her so? She remembered the night when she had found him, waiting in the dark, on her doorstep. He had said he didn't want to lose her. That was over six months ago. She had thought Henry was going to– Had she misread his intentions?

She took a deep breath.

He's just a friend, not–

The curtain flapped at her ear. She flicked the silk out of her hands. She was a professional, a respectable widow. Too old to act like a silly, infatuated girl. She scoffed at her lapse in rationality.

He's a colleague. That's all.

Footsteps approached along the hallway. A short rumble as a hatchway opened and closed. Crockery rattled in the corridor. A reedy tune whistled faintly through the keyhole.

Viola smiled. She could always rely on Polly to lift her spirits.

Tap. Tap.

Viola strode across the room toward the door. Polly! She'd know what's going on; why Henry left.

"Good morning, Miss Viola." Polly's cheerful voice rang though the room, as she opened the door.

Polly's eyes widened. She gasped and grabbed the teetering teacup. Liquid sloshed in the pot. Polly bobbed her greeting and cleared her throat.

"Breakfast in your rooms this morning, as requested." Polly eyed the dressing gown, its cord curling like a cat's tail and leading back toward the window.

Viola retreated from the doorway and reeled in the trailing cord.

Polly smiled, pushed the trolley across the room toward the window.

"Has Doctor Collins called yet?" asked Viola.

The rattling stopped.

"Cup of tea?" Polly removed the silver covers from the plates. The scrumptious smell of hot toast, eggs and fried mushrooms wafted on the breeze. All Viola's favourites.

"Were you expecting him before breakfast?"

Before breakfast? Viola shook her head. *But why did he leave without any greeting?*

"Doctor Collins will be attending luncheon," replied Viola calmly.

Polly opened the pear wood armoire and sifted through Viola's garments.

Viola breathed in the mouth-watering aroma of fresh toast. She dunked a corner into an egg yolk and crunched the flavoursome morsel. Delicious.

"Did he leave something for me?" asked Viola.

"No, Miss." Polly laid an emerald green skirt on the bed, next to Viola's petticoats, and teased out the pleats one by one.

Viola frowned and placed her fork back on the plate.

"Nothing at all?"

Polly placed a matching bodice on the bed beside the skirt.

"Sorry, Miss. Doctor Collins hasn't called yet today." She flicked fluff off the bodice collar. "But it is still early."

Viola eyed Polly as she lay out the clothes.

Why would Polly lie? The knock had been very quiet. It was still early. Polly would've been in the kitchen preparing her breakfast. Perhaps she hadn't heard Henry at the door? *Yes, that was it.*

Viola speared a juicy mushroom with her fork. The rich, earthy aroma tantalised her. She licked her lips. Field mushrooms were one of her favourites.

"I'll return when you've finished breakfast, Miss." Polly grabbed the door handle and curtsied.

"Happy birthday, Miss Viola."

The door clicked behind her.

The hall clock chimed twelve. Viola hovered on the hall stairs. She descended to the bottom step and waited for the doorbell to ring.

A jolly humming drifted from the dining room into the front hall. Viola's heart skipped. Had Henry already arrived?

Viola pinched her cheeks. Finally, she would discover why Henry aborted his morning visit - and why Polly was being so evasive.

I wonder where he'll take me after luncheon? It was such a glorious spring day, perfect for a walk in London Zoo. Viola clapped her hands together silently. *Or perhaps the new exhibits at Madame Tussaud's?*

Viola peered into the hall mirror and patted a few errant ringlets back into place. She took a deep breath, pulled the hem of her bodice taut and drifted through the doorway into the dining room.

"Henry, I–"

Polly stopped humming, straightened the silverware, and glanced up from setting the table. Her gaze flicked back to the silverware. She straightened them again.

"Luncheon will be ready in fifteen minutes, Miss."

Polly lifted a glass to the light and examined it as she turned it slowly, avoiding eye contact. She smiled and placed it on the crisp white cloth, to the right above the gilt-edged china plate.

Viola scanned the table. An elegant floral display of pink roses and gypsophila trailed along the centre. Her heart fluttered despite her attempts to remain calm.

Viola could feel the warmth spread up her neck. She cleared her throat.

"When does Doctor Collins arrive?" she asked.

A bell echoed in the hallway.

Polly put down the glass, straightened her apron and went to answer the doorbell.

Footsteps thunked down the hallway to the dining room door. Viola spun on her heel.

"Good afternoon, Doctor Stewart." Sir Archibald Huntington-Smythe stood in the doorway - hat in one hand, a brightly coloured parcel in the other. "And happy birthday, I understand."

Viola's cheeks warmed.

"Thank you, Sir Archibald."

He passed his hat to Polly and approached Viola.

Polly curtsied and glanced at the mantelpiece clock. A wrinkle flashed across her forehead.

"Shall I set another place, Miss?"

"Doctor Collins sends his most sincere apologies."

Viola's heart clenched. Was Henry avoiding her? She breathed deeply. Slowly. A lady must maintain her composure in all situations.

"He's been called out on an emergency. I dare say he is not happy with the situation but such is the life of a doctor, I'm afraid. Thank heavens my patients generally keep more civil hours."

Remain calm. Viola decided she could not abide surprises. She raised an eyebrow.

"I volunteered to break the news." Sir Archibald sighed and continued, always being the one to linger with conversation. "I offer myself as a diversion until such time as he arrives." A smile flickered across his lips. He proffered her the parcel, elegantly wrapped in patterned silk and tied with a yellow ribbon. "And present you with a birthday gift as compensation for any inconvenience I may cause."

"Thank you, Sir Archibald." The smooth silk slipped into her fingers. Viola examined the wrappings. "How intriguing."

Sir Archibald smiled.

"It's an oriental custom, I believe. The wrapping should be as pleasing as the gift it conceals."

Viola's eye widened. Perhaps she was a bit hasty about her judgement on surprises? She gestured toward the dining table.

"I would be honoured if you would stay for luncheon," she said.

Sir Archibald nodded his head in a bow.

"Dear Lady, how could I refuse?" He slapped his hands together. "Collins tells me to ensure I stay for cake."

The front doorbell clanged in the hall. Viola raised her eyes from the vestiges of salmon croquettes, partridge on toast, Charlotte russe and apple meringue.

Sir Archibald settled his wine glass on the table, flicked open his pocket watch and smiled.

Viola caught her breath. She picked up her napkin, dabbed the corners of her mouth and meticulously folded the linen next to her plate, hoping Sir Archibald had not noticed her excitement.

She would remain calm. All day she'd jumped each time the doorbell rang. Not this time. She had her own house, a guaranteed income, intellectual interests, loyal friends and an excellent library. She was an independent woman. And she was content. Her life did not require the validation of a man.

Polly entered the dining room.

"Doctor Collins to see you, Miss." Polly glanced in Sir Archibald's direction.

Viola's hands twitched. She dropped them into her lap and clasped them tight.

Slowly. Breathe slowly.

Henry glided into the room, looking exceedingly dapper in his high-buttoned vest and cravat. He ran his fingers through his tousled dark hair, straightened his coat. The door clicked shut behind him.

"I do apologise for being tardy. I trust I'm not too late for cake?"

Viola shook her head and rose from the table; her skirt tugged on the tablecloth as she moved away from the table to greet Henry.

"Is everything sorted, Collins?" asked Sir Archibald as he rose to his feet.

"Yes," replied Henry as he approached the dining table.

"Excellent," said Sir Archibald.

Henry strode toward Viola.

Viola drew a slow breath, and waited. She wanted nothing more than to throw her arms around him...

Not here. Not now. And not in front of company, even such a close friend as Sir Archibald. She clenched her hands tighter. She needed no man.

Viola bit her lip.

Just breathe.

"It's a pleasure to have your company, Doctor Collins." Viola raised her hand and smiled. He smelled of new leather, vanilla and spices. Viola raised an eyebrow. With a hint of mechanical oil. She breathed deeply.

Calm.

Henry gently clasped her fingers. His lips brushed against her hand. Viola's hand tingled.

"The pleasure is mine." Henry released his hold and bowed his head.

Viola's heart shrank in her chest. She withdrew her hand and closed it slowly. It seems she had misread his intentions.

"I trust Sir Archibald has kept you entertained with tedious and detailed descriptions of his latest toys?"

Viola nodded.

"I hope you behaved yourself, Archie?" said Henry.

"He was a perfect gentleman," said Viola. "As expected."

"I've been barely tolerable company, Collins. I'm sure Doctor Stewart would have preferred the company of her good friend."

Viola's cheeks flushed hot. "Sir Archibald, I hope I didn't–." She cleared her throat. "I didn't mean to–"

"Tut, tut, girl." Sir Archibald grinned. "I'm only teasing. Surely we can be less formal? After all, we have no secrets. I've seen your laboratory."

Viola glanced at Henry and straightened her skirts. Henry ran his finger along his moustaches, making a poor attempt to conceal his smile.

Sir Archibald rang the service bell.

Henry leaned toward Viola and lowered his voice.

"Sir Archibald likes you." Henry's moustache twitched.

Sir Archibald likes me! Viola's peered sideways at Henry and huffed. The door opened.

"Champagne for our honoured hostess!" Sir Archibald waved Polly into the room.

Sir Archibald spoke his mind. He treated her as an equal. While his etiquette was unconventional, she appreciated the sentiment.

"He's just being..." She glanced in Sir Archibald's direction. He was lecturing Polly on how to pour the champagne.

"–Sir Archibald," they said in unison.

Viola laughed softly, trying not to let Sir Archibald hear her.

Henry's eyes sparkled. Viola swallowed. A change of subject was required.

"He gave me a gift," whispered Viola.

Henry's gaze fell to Viola's décolletage.

She caught her finger around the gold chain around her neck, and lifted the new pendant to a less inappropriate distance for Henry to examine in company.

A large oval locket, its engraved filigree designs accentuated with flecks of brilliant amethyst, dangled from the chain. Three small triangular shaped gems protruded from the top of the pendant. Viola pinched one of the gems and drew out a long stiletto-shaped pin.

"It's ingenious." She placed the pin in Henry's palm. "A set of jewelled lock picks," she cooed.

"Very ingenious." Henry raised an eyebrow. "So, you now have a Lord facilitating your detectiving. As if you needed more encouragement?" He glanced in Sir Archibald's direction and back to the pin. He cradled the pendant in his hand, eased the pin home and lowered the pendant until it rested against her bodice.

Blood thumped through Viola's chest. The pendant bounced, keeping time with each heartbeat.

"Unique," he said. "I see I shall have to work hard to outdo Sir Archibald's present."

Viola's cheeks burned. She glanced across the room. Polly was still fussing with the glasses. Sir Archibald loosed the bottle's cork. It popped with a fizz. He poured the champagne and raised the glass in her direction.

"You've brought me something?" she asked Henry.

"Yes." Henry's hand retreated. "Would you like to see it?"

Viola nodded.

He caught Viola's hand and escorted her into the hall.

"Then close your eyes, Viola."

Viola closed her eye.

Click.

Viola felt a gentle breeze on her cheek. Henry's arm slipped around her elbow. She was escorted forward.

One step.

Two steps.

Three.

The door closed behind her. A warm breath caressed her ear.

"Happy birthday, Viola," he whispered. "Open your eyes."

Viola's eyelid crept open. Before her was an over-sized, lop-sided bundle of crisp white sheets, as tall as she, trussed up with red ribbons. She raised an eyebrow.

"A piano?" she asked. "But I don't play. Do you intend to pay for the lessons?"

Henry tipped his head to one side.

"It'd be a poor excuse for a piano," he replied. "Guess again."

Viola eyed the gargantuan parcel of cotton and silk. A ruby-red bow of titanic proportions confronted her. She took a step back. Her fingers twitched as she examined the sharp bulges and rounded corners on one side.

It resembled a miniature version of...

The creases melted away from her forehead. Her eye widened.

A scanning telescope? Not as large as Sir Archibald's of course.

Viola grinned and tugged one tail of the bow.

But why set it up in the hall?

The silk slipped through its knot and the ribbon trickled to the floor. Viola pinched a section of sheet and rubbed the cloth between her fingers. Viola pursed her lips and glared at Henry.

"My best Egyptian cotton sheets?" *No wonder Polly had been evasive all afternoon.* "Did you engage my maid in your subterfuge?"

"Only the best for you, Viola," Henry grinned back.

Viola licked her lips, grabbed the cloth and flicked it off the intrigue. The sheet billowed and slumped, but not before Viola caught a glimpse of a metal lever. She yanked the cloth free with a long rip.

Henry winced. "I'll replace them," he said.

Brass spokes glinted in the over-sized wheels on the back axle of the contraption. A third spoked wheel, half the size of its fellows but equally shiny, sat at the front. On a red, leather-padded seat lay a posie of heartsease, and white violets surrounding a single bright-red rose in full bloom.

Viola scooped up the posie and knelt on the seat to examine the contraption. Behind the seat was a large box, painted with blue and yellow scrollwork, with a built-in backrest of deep-upholstered leather, matching that of the seat. Under the seat was a small engine box. A brightly painted funnel pointed away from the engine behind the machine.

Viola sniffed the posie, the smell overpowered by that of new leather and motor oil. She placed the posie on the hall side table, not taking her attention from her prize.

"A motorised plectocycle?" Viola licked her lips and ran her fingers over the rim of a back wheel.

Freedom.

"With front steering and gears apparently," replied Henry.

"It's such an expensive gift, Henry. I can't possibly –"

Henry placed a finger against her lips and slipped his other hand into his coat pocket.

"Now you won't have to wait in the dark for a carriage when you gallivant around in the middle of the night," said Henry. "Think of it as my insurance you will return home safely."

Viola climbed into the contraption, plopped onto the plectocycle's seat and wrapped her fingers around the lever controls on either side of her.

She closed her eyes, remembering the rush of exhilaration when she had first driven Sir Archibald's motorwagon. Now she could ride alone. Independence. No restrictions. No–

Viola jumped off the seat, and kissed Henry on the cheek.

"It's perfect!" She spun towards the dining room, grabbed the door handle and flung open the door.

Henry's fingers searched his pocket and curled around their objective. He glanced at the posie on the side table. Henry's moustache drooped.

"Sir Archibald, come see the wondrous present Doctor Collins has given me."

Viola grinned and gesticulated enthusiastically toward the plectocycle, seemingly oblivious to his posie declaration. Yet she seemed ecstatic, almost floating across the tiled floor.

Henry's fingers froze. What if she rejected him?

Sir Archibald's head popped through the doorway. He pushed his spectacles up his nose and examined the plectocycle.

"Well done, Collins. It puts my trinket to shame." Sir Archibald slapped Henry on the shoulder, as he balanced a full glass of champagne in the other hand.

Viola dropped her hands and spun to face the plectocycle.

"But I don't have papers!" she gasped.

Henry removed his hand from his pocket and flexed his fingers.

The moment was lost.

Sir Archibald delved his long, thin fingers into a coat pocket and produced a wad of tightly bound papers. He winked and presented them to Viola.

"Oh, thank you, Sir Archibald!" Viola cracked open the seal and unfolded the papers. A full set of Mechanical Ownership and Operation Permits. "But how –?" she asked.

"I was owed a favour and Collins here was very persuasive," replied Sir Archibald. He leaned closer to Henry. "All arranged?" he asked with a grin.

Henry glanced at the posie on the side table.

"Not exactly," he replied.

"I see." Sir Archibald's grin slipped.

They both watched Viola as she stuffed the folded permit under her bodice, snatched up a pair of leather riding gloves, and wheeled the plectocycle to the front door. She retrieved her tinted spectacles from the side table drawer, slipped them over her eye patch and adjusted the side shields in position.

"You'll get another opportunity," whispered Sir Archibald.

Henry bit his lip. Would he? The ring weighed heavy in his pocket. He had seen the same expression on Viola's face when she had graduated. Freedom. Independence. What could he offer her?

Viola tested the weight of the plectocycle and manoeuvred it through the front door and down the step. She squirmed as she twiddled knobs and pulled the lever by the seat.

Henry smiled. Viola was happy.

Gears clicked and whirred. Steam hissed from the engine box.

She was finally free of her past. Free of a husband. She didn't need anyone.

His moustache wilted. She didn't need him.

Henry stood at the threshold, his friend beside him. "What if I lose her, Archie?" he asked. "I've waited..." He took a deep breath. "Ten years is a long time."

Sir Archibald placed a hand on his shoulder. "She'll fly —" he chuckled. "But she'll return to you. Don't worry."

Henry regarded his friend. "I wish I had your confidence."

"I wish I had your conviction," said Sir Archibald.

Henry raised an eyebrow.

"You've opted to court a woman who doesn't need you, Collins." Sir Archibald handed Henry the glass.

Henry gulped down the champagne, ignoring the festive bubbles.

The engine chugged. Viola leaned into the seat. Her entire body vibrated. She pulled the right hand lever, then the left. The front wheel turned one way then the other. Her pulse raced. Her nerves tingled.

Polly rushed up to Viola and thrust a hat in her direction.

"I don't know what they were thinking, them being doctors too. You can't go without your hat, Miss Viola."

Viola nodded.

"Thank you, Polly."

Viola glanced back to her house. Henry and Sir Archibald stood in the doorway, deep in conversation. Henry returned her gaze, smiled and sipped champagne. He seemed content. Sir Archibald chuckled.

I wish I knew what you were thinking, Henry Collins.

A particularly large puff of steam exploded around her. The plectocycle shuddered.

Polly jumped clear and edged back to the footpath. She glanced over the plectocycle and straightened her apron.

"Will you be home for supper, Miss?" asked Polly.

"I'm not entirely sure." Viola grinned and pulled her driving gloves snug. "Make sure they don't drink all of the champagne while I'm gone."

THE END

Point of View

T he smell of fresh-baked sugar biscuits and nutmeg suffused the kitchen. Baking trays clattered on the bench. Water gurgled in the kettle. Its whistle chirped and warbled and crescendoed into a high-pitched scream.

Polly grabbed a cloth, rescued the kettle and set it on the wooden sideboard. She swirled and decanted the cooling water from the waiting teapot, dropped a few teaspoons of Assam tea and finally poured the steaming water into the pot.

Constable Cooper popped his head through the open window.

"I'd love a cup, Polly." He removed his custodian helmet and smiled.

Polly snatched up the cloth and snapped it in the direction of the window.

Cooper flinched, hesitated, then leaned in further.

"Are they fresh biscuits?" He nodded his head in the direction of the trays full of steaming delights.

The constable closed his eyes, inhaled deeply and licked his lips. His eyes snapped open.

"They smell almost as divine as their creator." He winked as his hand crept toward the trays.

Polly slapped his hand.

"Just as well I baked extra," she said.

"Don't you always?" said Cooper.

The corner of Polly's mouth curled. She cleared her throat.

"Go on. But you'd better have interesting news for me." Polly poured the Constable a cup of tea.

The tray rattled beside her. She turned to find the Constable crunching on a biscuit.

"George Cooper, you scoundrel!" replied Polly. "They're for the

Mistress and Doctor Collins."

"Any progress there?" asked the Constable.

"No." Polly puffed her cheeks and huffed. "Propriety makes for a tortuous, and tedious, courtship."

"I've heard Lady Calthorpe cannot contain herself." He sipped his tea. "Her maid says she prattles on about appearances and her strenuous efforts at curtailing salacious gossip."

Polly sighed as she topped up the teapot.

"I do worry for Miss Viola. Those that don't know her won't understand the situation." She turned to face the Constable and fluttered her lashes. "I'm sure you wouldn't keep your sweetheart waiting, George."

George gulped his tea and smiled.

"Not if I had the means to guarantee the capture, Polly." He filched another biscuit from the tray. "Or had no rival." He nibbled on his biscuit. "How is your friend, Mr Mercer?"

"I'm sure you can ask *Benjamin* yourself. I'm expecting a delivery for Miss Viola's laboratory this morning." Polly piled warm biscuits on a plate and placed it on a silver tray next to the teapot.

"*Benjamin*, now, is it?" His cup tinked the saucer.

"Behave, Constable Cooper, or you may find there's no supper for you next time you stroll by my window."

"Propriety does make for a tedious courtship." George narrowed his eyelids. "I suppose there's biscuits for Mercer as well?"

Polly leaned forward and gently wiped crumbs from the corner of George's mouth. "Not if you give me a good reason," she whispered.

George's eyes widened.

"I'm up for promotion soon and the Superintendent is putting in a good word for me." He puffed out his chest and leaned closer. "I'll be able to–"

A bell trilled above their heads.

George frowned.

Polly sighed.

"That'll be Benjamin, with the delivery," said Polly, as she placed a clean cheesecloth over the tea tray.

"Off with you, Constable Cooper. You have a beat to plod." Polly waved him away.

George checked his tarnished silver pocket watch. He shook his head.

"I have some time before I'm due at the station," he said. "I'm not going anywhere until I finally spy the competition." He snatched another biscuit off the cooling tray near the sill and popped it in his mouth.

Polly narrowed her eyelids and jerked on the bottom of the open window sash. George jumped clear and grumbled. He hovered for a moment, slapped his helmet on his head and edged back into the bushes surrounding the kitchen garden.

The bell trilled again. Polly wiped her hands on her apron before pulling the pendant chain by the service door. The chain rattled as it snapped back in place. A grinding noise echoed across the back yard as the gate rolled open.

Polly peered through the window glass. Steam puffed skyward near the hinges of the carriage gate. A glistening grey trotted into the yard and clopped to a halt.

She flipped a lever on the wall. Gears groaned under her feet and in the wall, as the ascension box trundled up from Miss Viola's laboratory. It was just one of the many instalments over the past few months.

Polly closed her eyes as she wiped her hands on her apron and listened as the ascension box chugged closer. She loved the sound. Life was easier now Miss Viola had Mechanical Ownership and Operation Permits. No more lugging of supplies or late night suppers up and down to the laboratory.

Stones crunched in the yard. Trolley wheels squeaked closer.

Polly tucked a stray tendril of hair behind her ear, straightened her apron and pinched her cheeks. She strode to the door and opened it with a grin.

"Benjamin–!"

An unfamiliar face stared back at her, framed by a pile of crates on a hand trolley - pale eyes and hair squashed under a grey tweed cap. A dusky woollen scarf wound high around his neck, covering his chin.

"Good afternoon, miss. I have a delivery for Doctor Stewart."

Polly cleared her throat.

"Where's Mr Mercer?" she asked.

"Mr Mercer has been called out of London. I'm doing deliveries today." His voice was muffled.

"And you are?"

"Mr Umber at your service." He tipped his hat.

"I do hope it's nothing serious?" said Polly.

"Death in the family." The trolley's wheels knocked the step. Umber scanned the kitchen.

"It's a big order," he said. "I'll take it down to the laboratory for you."

The wall whirred. The ascension box clunked to a halt. Umber's gaze flicked toward the hatch on the wall.

"There's no need." Polly rotated the wall lever. A window-sized hatch ratcheted open, revealing a wall cavity. Ropes slid over pulleys in the shadows.

Umber glared at the box.

Polly scrutinised the interloper as he ferried the crates to the box and they waited for the ascension box to return. His gaze darted over the room and along the hallway. He peered into the bowels of the ascension shaft, as if he hadn't seen a mechanical before.

"Problem?" she asked.

"No." Umber's eyelids relaxed. "I wasn't informed Doctor Stewart had permits for domestic mechanicals," he replied as he pushed the last crate into the box.

"Doctor Stewart is well-respected, Mr Umber. Patronised by gentry, with excellent connections."

Polly crossed her arms. *He is nosey for a substitute delivery man.*

"When did you say Mr Mercer will return?" she asked.

"I didn't," replied Umber. "I can see you're busy with company expected. I'll show myself out."

He strode to the door, stumbled on the threshold and fell against the door frame, catching his foot against his trolley.

"Are you hurt?" Polly asked as she stepped forward and unfolded her arms. She eyed his feet. A large chunk had been gouged in the previously pristine leather of his immaculate shoes.

Umber straightened his shoulders, tipped his cap, and stepped into the yard.

The bushes rustled as the door shut with a click.

Polly shut the wall hatch and pushed down the wall lever.

"I need a cup of tea," she said.

A lively conversation bubbled through the dining room.

Polly hovered near the front windows, waiting for her mistress and Doctor Collins to finish their mains - snipes in savoury jelly, roast hare with fennel, squash and stewed mushroom. She examined the wallpaper, tracing the acanthus up and around the carved frames of each painting toward the ceiling. She counted the bosses on the moulding, trying to distract herself from accidentally eavesdropping on Miss Viola's latest tale of detectiving.

Doctor Collins glanced at Viola and smiled. He stretched out his hand, almost touching her fingers. A smile flickered across her lips. She glanced at the table, lingering on the mushrooms.

"Viola, I have something important to say," said Doctor Collins in a lowered voice.

Finally! Polly counted the bosses in earnest, as she turned her ear toward the dining table.

The window vibrated. Outside the wind howled.

His hand snapped back to his wine glass.

Soft velvet fluttered across Polly's neck. She tucked the curtain behind her and bit her lip, resisting the urge to groan. It had been six months since Miss Viola's birthday. Polly had seen the carefully chosen posie – heartsease, white violets and a single red rose. *In full bloom.* The man was smitten. It was obvious. So, why was it taking so long for him to declare himself?

A stream of air chilled Polly's arm. The wind had been blowing from the North all morning.

"The chill is starting early," said Miss Viola.

"The newspapers say it could last longer than first expected." Doctor Collins picked up his glass and sipped his Madeira.

A soft chink of cutlery on an empty plate signalled Polly. She approached the table.

"Shall I light the fire, Miss?" asked Polly as she picked up her mistress's plate.

"Thank you, Polly." Miss Viola nodded and fidgeted with her napkin.

The cutlery rattled as she deposited it on the side table. Polly lit a match and snapped open the air vents. She held out the match to check the air current, then slapped the damper shut. The flame flickered higher, toward the chimney. She pressed the match into the kindling in the fireplace.

"They've taken Doyle to the Station, for questioning," whispered Doctor Collins.

Miss Viola gasped.

"Not Arthur? He was helping them with the investigation." Her hands thudded softly on the table. "Surely they can't think he had anything to do with the Superintendent's death?"

The match shook in Polly's hand, its heat singed her fingers.

Not Doctor Doyle? She loved his stories. She dropped the match and breathed on the unsteady flames.

A glass clinked against metal.

"That is precisely why they suspect him," he replied.

Polly gathered up the edges of her apron, grasped a small log and placed it on the bed of kindling. The fire licked the edges and danced across the blackened wood.

"What motive could he possibly have?" asked Miss Viola. "He and the Superintendent were friends. They played on the same cricket team."

Polly peered into the growing flames and frowned. Doctor Doyle was always polite when he visited. He didn't look like a murderer. He even liked her ginger cake. Surely, Doctor Collins was misinformed? Polly turned her ear toward the dining table and poked the kindling.

"Viola." Doctor Collins leaned closer to Miss Viola and spoke in a hushed voice. "He was seen leaving the alley just before the murder was discovered. There are several witnesses."

Viola shook her head.

"No, I can't believe it. He wouldn't–. There must be some mistake."

Polly bit her tongue. But he had such kind eyes.

"I've seen the statement, Viola," said Doctor Collins. "And the body. The killer had medical knowledge."

"So do I. You, too, Henry. Will they arrest us as well?"

"Viola, don't be–"

The room was silent.

Polly swallowed. No more stories? She replaced the poker and straightened up.

"Will there be anything else, Miss?"

Viola glanced in Polly's direction. The frown lingered only a second before the lines disappeared from her forehead. Her crinkled lip slowly lifted.

"No, thank you, Polly." Viola silently placed her cutlery on the plate.

"I think we're finished."

Polly curtsied. She collected the plates. The stacked crockery chinked as she closed the dining room behind her.

The smell of Darjeeling and fresh pastries filled the hallway. The studio bell dinged again. Polly quickened her pace. No doubt Lady Calthorpe was getting jittery, having had to sit still for over an hour.

"Oh, but I insist." The muffled voice leaked through the parlour door.

Polly gripped the tea tray and nudged the door open with her hip. She curtsied, taking care not to unbalance the pot.

Lady Calthorpe's bonnet bobbed, her jewelled hatpins danced in time with her hand gestures.

"It's a brand new exhibit." Lady Calthorpe lowered her voice. "And I dare not enter without an escort. All those wax effigies. It's as if you were looking at your very own doppelganger." She shivered. "It's unnerving, especially after that nasty business with the exhibit's previous artist."

Lady Calthorpe clutched at her chest and shook her head.

"My heart shouldn't stand it, if I were to go alone, without your company. You must come, Doctor Stewart. What if I should have a fit of the vapours?"

Wooden handles clicked as Miss Viola swapped paintbrushes. She nodded slowly and waved Polly closer.

Polly entered the studio. The rich smell of linseed oil and fresh paint enveloped her.

Lady Calthorpe sat in state amongst a throne of over-stuffed and over-embroidered cushions, her face lifted toward an unseen prize and one hand raised in aggrandisement.

Polly bit her lip and tilted her head to one side, trying to spy the painting in progress. She slipped the tea tray onto a work table, jostling one of the containers. Coloured water swirled in the glass. The acrid tang of turpentine caught her nostrils. Her eyes watered. She steadied the glass and edged it to a safer distance.

Serves me right for snooping.

The wall clock chimed. Lady Calthorpe glanced at the tea tray and frowned.

"Doctor Doyle should be arriving soon. He agreed to join us on our Wax Works adventure." Lady Calthorpe's nose twitched. She sighed and dropped her arm into her lap. "I understand he is writing another book. Lord Calthorpe found his first mildly diverting."

"Doctor Doyle was coming with us to Madame Tussaud's?" asked Viola.

"Yes. I've arranged for him to meet us here. I do hope I haven't inconvenienced you."

Miss Viola lowered her gaze.

"Then you haven't heard?"

Polly laid out tea cups and poured some tea. It was strange Lady Calthorpe hadn't heard the news; it mustn't be common knowledge yet.

"Heard what, my dear Doctor Stewart?" Lady Calthorpe rose from her chair; cushions rained silently to the studio floor.

"I fear Doctor Doyle is unavoidably detained."

Polly poured a second cup of tea.

"I do hope it's nothing serious," said Lady Calthorpe.

Miss Viola's paintbrush clicked on the easel shelf.

"He's being questioned at Marylebone Police Station, with regards to the Superintendent's murder."

"There must be some mistake." Lady Calthorpe raised an eyebrow. "I shall have to have a word with the Inspector." She cleared her throat and straightened her skirts. "Well, we can't let that spoil our outing." She turned to Polly. "Fetch your Mistress' coat."

"Yes, Your Ladyship." Polly covered the tea tray and curtsied. The studio door clicked shut behind her.

Sunlight spilled through the stained glass side lights on either side of the front door, glared off the hall floor tiles, and reflected a kaleidoscoped chequer-board across the wall near the hall stairs.

Polly fetched Miss Viola's favourite blue velvet *visite* with Chinese knot buttons and folded it over one arm. She paused near a side light, peered through the glass and pursed her lips.

Midday.

She couldn't let Miss Viola get too much sun. She snatched up a parasol from the hall stand and returned to the studio.

She could hear Lady Calthorpe's muffled voice on the other side of the door:

"I've already ordered the carriage. And besides, we both deserve a treat after this morning's hard work."

Polly knocked, waited a moment and opened the door. She stepped aside as Lady Calthorpe bustled past her into the hall. Miss Viola rolled her eyes in Polly's direction, as she followed. Polly bit her lip. They both knew it was much less effort to acquiesce to Lady Calthorpe's whims.

Miss Viola eyed her parasol and smiled.

"What would I do without you, Polly?" she whispered.

Polly smiled. She held out the *visite* and slipped it around Miss Viola's shoulders.

Lady Calthorpe had barely made it past the hall stairs when she stopped mid-step.

"That can't be correct," she mumbled. She spun on her heel.

"What was the date of the unfortunate man's demise?" she asked.

Viola looked at her blankly, mouth open as she tugged on a pair of kid gloves.

"Come on, girl. When was the Superintendent murdered?"

"The thirteenth," replied Miss Viola.

Lady Calthorpe's eyes narrowed. She shook her head.

"Then they have the wrong man," she said.

Polly grinned. *I knew it!*

"The Constabulary have a witness." Miss Viola slid on her tinted spectacles.

"Doctor Doyle did not murder anyone. And I can prove it." Lady Calthorpe turned to face Miss Viola. "Lord Calthorpe and I ate supper at The Langham on the thirteenth. Doctor Doyle was dining with two gentlemen – that scandalous poet and an American, I think. They were there all evening."

Lady Calthorpe extricated her gloves from her purse.

"That makes me a witness, doesn't it?" She pulled on the gloves and pushed down between the fingers. "If we hurry, we can stop by Marylebone Station on the way to Madame Tussaud's."

Polly dunked the corner of the rag into vinegar, wrapped it around her finger and scraped at a blackberry stain on the kitchen bench. The last remnants were always the most difficult to remove. She leaned closer and scrutinised the wood. Barely a trace left. Her eyelids relaxed.

"That's better," she said.

Window glass tapped behind her.

Polly glanced at the clock on the wall. Right on time. She slowly unwound the cloth, smiled and dusted off her bodice and apron.

"Good morning, Constable Cooper." She turned toward the half-open window.

The Constable licked his lips and scanned the kitchen.

Polly strolled over to the window and pushed it open. A weight clunked inside the frame. The bouquet of crushed lavender and mint hovered in the air.

Polly slapped a cloth onto the windowsill.

George flinched. "What was that for?" he sputtered.

"Constable George Cooper, you've been trampling on my kitchen garden again."

He slinked away from the window, straightened his helmet and lowered his gaze.

Polly bit the inside of her lip, stifling a grin.

"I don't suppose there are any blackberry tarts left?" asked George.

"Too late." Polly shook her head. "I've just taken Doctor Stewart and Miss Blake their morning tea."

George's shoulders slumped.

"But I may be able to find something..." Polly leaned on the windowsill. "If you have any exciting news to share."

George picked his way back through the herbs to the kitchen window.

"I spied that new delivery man entering Doctor Stewart's clinic."

"Mr Umber?" Polly wrinkled her eyebrow.

George nodded and leaned closer to Polly. "Is Doctor Stewart constructing a new invention?"

"Large deliveries are supposed to come here, not the Clinic."

"He didn't have any boxes," said George. "Maybe he had an appointment?"

"He couldn't afford–" The warmth drained from Polly's face. An appointment would cost more than those shiny new...

"His shoes!" She dropped her cloth.

"Shoes?" asked George.

"He was wearing new shoes. Expensive ones." Polly threw off her apron and grabbed George's arm. "A delivery man can't afford shoes like that." She spun on her heel, and bolted toward the door. "Meet me at the Clinic!"

She fumbled with the handle, flung open the door and dashed down the narrow service corridor toward Miss Viola's clinic.

The click of the door echoed through the waiting room. Polly's boots clicked on the parquetry floor. The wall clock ticked. The chairs were empty. There was no other sound. And no Miss Blake to scold Polly for bursting into the Clinic unannounced.

Polly peeked around the corner toward Miss Blake's desk, which guarded the testing rooms.

A mop of blonde hair lay on the desk, a loose tendril soaking in a pool of Darjeeling. Miss Blake's finger still curled through the handle of her overturned teacup. Polly's heart skipped.

Miss Blake would never sleep on the job.

Polly rushed to the desk. She held her hand under Miss Blake's nose. *Nothing.* Polly shivered.

What was it that Doctor Collins did to check for a pulse? She swallowed, wiggled her fingers and placed them against Miss Blake's neck.

Still nothing. She swallowed and repositioned her fingers. There. A faint thump flickered under her finger tips. Polly took a deep breath. Her heart slowed.

She extracted Miss Blake's finger from the handle and lifted the tea cup to her nostrils.

Sickly sweet with a hint of spices and wax. Polly wrinkled her nose. *Drugged?*

A muffled thunk emanated from the testing room. Something fell.

Polly flinched. The cup slipped from her fingers and smashed onto the floor.

The noises stopped.

Miss Viola! Polly swallowed, picked up the letter opener from the desk and tiptoed to the door.

What was taking George so long? She bit her lip as she turned the door knob.

Click. Polly nudged the door open a crack.

A bundle of emerald silk skirts lay crumpled on the floor. A matching eye patch lay a few inches from the bundle.

Glass crashed.

Polly's eyes snapped shut. She slammed her body back against the wall, swung her arm up to shield her face and brandished the letter opener against any impending onslaught.

A flurry of wind tugged at her sleeve. Glass tinkled on the street outside.

Polly peeked over her arm. The bundle twitched and groaned, amongst a sea of scattered metal-rimmed lenses. One skittered across the floor, knocking into an upturned lens case and ricocheted into a chair leg.

Polly's heart jumped.

"Miss Viola!" Glass crunched underfoot as Polly launched herself toward her Mistress, and rolled her foot over something in the debris. She fell to her knees by the bundle and reached for the offending object – a metal syringe with smears of wax on the plunger. Polly caught her breath.

Please, no...

She shook the syringe. There was a reassuring slosh of liquid. Polly sighed.

Perhaps she's not–

The bundle rustled. A pale arm reached out. Polly gasped.

She's alive!

Miss Viola moaned, rolled onto her side and cracked open her eye.

"Did you get him?" she asked.

"No, Miss," replied Polly, as she pointed to the shattered window. "He must have jumped."

"Did he escape?" asked Viola.

Polly hauled herself to her feet and picked her way through the optical lenses toward the window, syringe still in hand. She brushed glass shards from the sill and leaned out.

One of the potted topiaries lay on the step, the pot cracked. Dark earth spilled down the pale steps. A trail of dirt led along the street.

Running footsteps faded into the distance. A second set of footfalls raced out of the alley. George raced to the front steps, brandishing his truncheon.

"George, up here."

George steadied his helmet and craned his neck to view the window.

"What happened?" he asked, as his foot slipped on the loose earth.

"The delivery man attacked Doctor Stewart. He escaped through the window. He went that way." Polly pointed in the direction of the retreating footsteps. "Catch him!"

George nodded. His boots clicked on the cobblestones as he sped off in pursuit.

A soft murmur redirected Polly's attention to her Mistress. She helped Miss Viola to her feet.

"Are you injured, Miss?" she asked.

Viola hauled herself up and leaned on the knuckles of one hand. She swayed precariously and grabbed her forehead with her free hand.

"Only my pride." Her voice was weak.

Polly slipped one hand under her Mistress' arm, slipped the other around her waist, and escorted her to the testing chair.

"Doctor Collins will never let me hear the end of this," whispered Miss Viola. She eased into the chair and cradled her head in her hands. "Miss Blake... Is she–?"

"Miss Blake is alive. Drugged, I think," replied Polly. "I'll fetch Doctor Collins to look after her." Polly handed Viola her eye patch.

A shutter rattled. Polly glanced toward the shattered window and frowned.

"I don't understand. Why did the delivery man attack you?" asked Polly.

"He wasn't a delivery man," replied Viola. She presented her closed hand, the knuckles now blanched, and unfurled her fingers. A silver, cog-shaped badge glistened in the sunlight. A brass ouroboros curled around its circumference.

Polly wrinkled her eyebrow. *What did it mean?*

"That was a Man in Grey. And he was in my house," hissed Viola.

The smell of fresh bread had dwindled hours ago. Whiffs of steam escaped from the kettle. Polly yawned and closed her book. The kitchen chair scraped on the stone tiles as she rose and tucked the book under her arm.

Time for bed.

She closed her eyes and took a deep breath. It had been a long day. Miss Viola had missed supper again. She was off detectiving, with her cohorts in tow. Without her warm gloves. Polly frowned. And no notice on how late she would be. It could be hours before they returned.

Polly eyed the supper plates on the bench. Miss Viola will be starving when she returns. Polly shook her head and reached for her lamp.

A clatter echoed along the service corridor, outside the kitchen.

Her hand froze.

Perhaps Miss Viola and her party had finally returned, already victorious?

A floor board creaked in the distance.

But they would arrive via the front door, never the servant's entrance.

Polly twisted the knob on the lamp. The oil flame flickered and shrivelled in the darkness. She crept up to the kitchen door, pushed it open – just a crack – and peered along the dark corridor.

Nothing.

She held her breath as her eyes adjusted to the gloom.

Still nothing.

Old houses complain in the night. That was it. Her shoulders relaxed as she let out her breath slowly.

A faint clinking trickled down from the front rooms. Polly's heart thumped. That wasn't the house complaining. Perhaps a window was left open?

Clink.

Polly extracted the book from under her arm and hefted it in her hand.

Miss Viola will scold me if I damage one of her books.

Polly unlaced her boots, slipped them off and placed them silently by the doorway as she scanned the kitchen benches for a weapon. Everything was tidied away. Too organised.

Botheration.

The new copper kettle glimmered in the moonlight. Polly wrapped her fingers around the handle and lifted it off the stove. Water sloshed.

Half full. She rested her palm against its side and grinned. And still hot.

Polly padded down the corridor, until she reached the entry door for the servant quarters. A draught danced around her ankles. Polly squinted. All was dark, and silent. She reached for the door. A breeze tickled her fingers. She traced the draught upwards, along the door frame.

Polly swallowed. The door was always closed. Her fingers trembled as she gripped the kettle.

Clink.

Someone was in the front hall. Polly's nails dug into the heel of her palm. She winced.

A board squeaked. Polly knew that sound. It always betrayed the Mistress when she tried to sneak out at night to go detectiving.

Polly's breath faltered.

He's on the stairs. Her muscles tensed. She took a slow, silent breath and edged the door open – just enough to slip into the hall.

Moonlight dribbled through the side lights into the hallway. Polly blinked as her eyes adjusted.

A trousered shadow limped on the stairs.

Polly crept along the wall, closer to her quarry. The figure grasped the bannister. She flattened her body against the wall, safe in the shadow of the stairs.

Water slapped in the kettle.

Polly grimaced and held her breath.

The figure climbed another step.

Creak.

It paused, scanned the landing above, then continued.

Polly exhaled. *It's now or never.* She gathered up her skirt, hitched it into her belt and inched along the edge of the stairs.

Now!

She sprang from the shadows, sprinted the remaining few steps and pounced onto the bottom stair, avoiding the Judas-floorboard. She raised the kettle - slosh - and slammed it into the back of the intruder's head, with a crack. Hot water spilled from the kettle and cascaded over his skin. The kettle lid clattered on the floor.

The intruder howled, arched his back and flailed in Polly's direction. Polly dodged, thudded her back onto the wall and raised the kettle, ready for a retaliatory attack. His hand spasmed. He moaned as his body went limp and tumbled down the stairs.

Blood rushed through Polly's ears. Her ragged breath kept pace with the tick of the hall clock. She shook the kettle.

Almost empty. Too light to do any lasting damage. She dropped the kettle and groped at the hall stand until she found something solid. Her fingers wrapped around an old cane. She slid it out of the side box. It was top-heavy. Solid. She examined the head - a dragon. It had belonged to the late Master. Miss Viola had insisted on keeping it.

Tick.

Polly licked her lips and thwacked the cane into the intruder's stomach.

Tick.

No movement.

Tick. Tick.

She slowed her breaths.

Tick. Tick. Tick.

It was over.

The hall clock whirred in the shadows. The minute hand clicked and fell into place behind its partner.

Bong.

The chimes filled the hall. Polly counted them... eleven. Twelve. The gears whirred and settled into place.

Polly bit her lip.

Midnight. She wrung her hands until they throbbed.

Hooves clattered in the street. Closer. Scuffles and laughter accosted the front door.

The lock rattled.

Polly turned to the door and huffed. Not another one. She crouched and drew back the cane, ready to strike. Not in my house!

A thud on the door, followed by a scraping sound. Polly eyed the door.

Sounds like... claws? She hesitated.

"Careful, Sir Archibald." It was a familiar voice.

Miss Viola? The cane lowered.

Another long scrape. The cane froze.

"Those fingers are sharp," said Miss Viola. "How will I explain those scrapes to Lady Calthorpe?'

Polly frowned and retreated two steps. *Fingers?*

The door burst open. Laughter rang in Polly's ears. Three bodies bustled into the hall. First the Mistress - in a rustle and flurry of silk skirts and brandishing a crumpled bonnet. A jewelled hat pin hung precariously from her tousled coiffure. Miss Viola froze, on the threshold, mid-step. The hat pin wobbled and tinged on the tiled floor.

A tendril of hair tickled Polly's nose. She tucked it up behind her ear and relaxed her shoulders.

Miss Viola's eye widened.

"Polly, you're still awake?" she said.

Polly opened her mouth to reply. A cool breeze played around her shins. Her cheeks burned. She unhitched her skirts and yanked the hem toward the floor, and avoided Miss Viola's stare.

"Come on, Viola. We'll catch our death out here." Doctor Collins knocked his boots against the top step.

"Well, you will go jumping into lakes after submersibles," replied Sir Archibald.

Doctor Collins squeezed past Viola. Soggy clothes dripped onto the floor. The hall rug squelched under his feet.

"I can't wait to examine this beauty." Sir Archibald stepped into the breach, brandishing a severed mechanical arm. He slapped Doctor Collins' shoulder and grinned. "And report back to your lot, of course, Collins."

Metal rods and pulleys whirred and clacked as the limb jiggled in his hand. Wires clicked and lashed.

Doctor Collins glanced at the cane and raised an eyebrow. He sidestepped toward the hallstand, narrowly avoiding the flailing fingers of the disembodied arm. His gaze met Polly's. The eyebrow slipped – just a fraction. He cleared his throat. And stared.

"Good evening," he said.

Polly closed her mouth and blinked.

All three now stared at her, no, past her, in the direction of the crumpled mass of dark clothing at the foot of the stairs.

Doctor Collins strode up to the body, crouched down and checked for a pulse.

"He's alive."

Miss Viola relaxed. The mechanical arm flopped by Sir Archibald's side.

Doctor Collins turned the intruder onto his back. A pair of goggles covered almost half of his soot-daubed face. Thick lenses gave the appearance of massive fish-like eyes. Doctor Collins removed the goggles and tossed them to Miss Viola.

Polly peered at the intruder's face. She was certain it was the delivery man under all the grime. Her gaze tracked to his shoes. New leather... with a gouge in one toe.

"That's him!" Polly gasped.

"Who?" asked Doctor Collins.

"The Man in Grey who tried to kill me this morning," Miss Viola stepped closer to the body.

"Tried to–?" Doctor Collins stood slowly. His eyes narrowed. "... what?"

"I knew there was something odd about him," said Polly. "I didn't trust his shoes."

The detectiving party turned to Polly. She cleared her throat, stepped back toward the hallstand and slipped the cane home. It rattled against the parasols. Polly tugged the hem of her bodice taut, patted her skirts flat and curtsied in their direction.

"Would you like some tea?" she asked.

Doctor Collins leaned closer.

"And cake?" he asked with a wink.

"Yes, sir." Polly eyed the growing puddles on the floor.

"I think Doctor Collins may be in need of a towel," said Miss Viola.

Polly nodded. Tea, cake and towels. Typical day really.

A peal of revelry accompanied the co-conspirators as they poured into the Parlour.

"It's a pity the rest of the automaton was crushed under the engine," said Sir Archibald. "I say, you've got a very impressive maid there, Viola."

"I blame Doyle and those wretched detective books of his," said Doctor Collins.

Miss Viola's head peeked through the Parlour doorway. She handed Polly a cloth-wrapped parcel.

"Box this up," Miss Viola grinned. "A souvenir from Tussaud's, for

Doctor Doyle."

Polly peeled back the cloth and gasped. Grey glass eyes stared back from a waxen face; a perfect replica of the man.

"And call a Constable to alert the Station before you fetch the tea."

Polly stepped over the Man in Grey to retrieve the kettle. There was a sizable dent in the shiny copper. She rolled her eyes and strode from the hall.

Now I know how Watson feels.

THE END

Mars Ascending

Candlelight flickered over the crisp white tablecloth. Golden reflections danced in the silver plate. Flecks glinted in the dark marble mantelpiece. Black lacquered sideboards glistened.

Henry glanced along the dining table. He had not realised Lord and Lady Calthorpe were astronomy enthusiasts. Viola, of course, would never decline a chance to venture into Sir Archibald's observatory. Sir Archibald sat at the head of the table, gesticulating as he regaled his guests with yet another anecdote from his sojourn at the Paris World Fair.

"... an odious column of bolted metal. And then he left." Sir Archibald clapped his hands together.

Viola's eyes sparkled. Her lips parted as if to reply. She shook her head and laughed. Auburn curls danced around her face.

"He left?" said Viola.

Sir Archibald nodded.

"She would not have been pleased." Viola glanced in Henry's direction. A faint smile flickered over her lips.

Henry returned a smile as he lifted his napkin and dabbed his moustache.

A series of clicks joined the conversation. Henry's gaze flicked to Lord Calthorpe, sitting beside Viola. A whir, and his knife clattered onto his plate. Henry's smile faded.

"I do apologise, Sir Archibald." Lord Calthorpe slipped his hand under his napkin. The clicking continued. The napkin twitched. "I fear I may never master this..." He stared at the napkin. "... thing."

Lady Calthorpe reached across the table and patted the camouflaged mechanical.

"Patience, my dear. Sir Archibald said it will take time."

Lord Calthorpe frowned and slid his covered hand off the table.

"It's been two months," he grumbled.

"You *will* insist on attending the hunt, at your age," his wife replied.

"At my–?" Lord Calthorpe harrumphed. His hand whirred mercilessly under the table.

"Yes, at your age." Lady Calthorpe quietly placed her cutlery on her plate.

Henry bit his lip. Lord Calthorpe was not one to let anyone see him lose control.

"Relax. You'll have a better grip on the reins now," said Sir Archibald as he motioned to his butler.

"Don't encourage him, Sir Archibald." Lady Calthorpe pursed her lips, reminiscent of Henry's scolding nanny.

Lord Calthorpe glanced at his wife and chuckled. The whirring slowed.

"It's not your workmanship, Archibald. You've wasted your skills on me."

Lady Calthorpe glanced at her husband and frowned.

"Sir Archibald, can you explain again what the Mars periapsis is? I get all muddled when it comes to astronomy."

Henry smiled. An obvious subject change but effective. Lord Calthorpe's hand silenced.

"It marks the point in Mars' orbit where it is closest to the Earth, affording an excellent view of its surface," replied Sir Archibald.

The Dining room door opened. A compact cart trundled and hissed across the carpet and halted at one end of the table. Small puffs of steam

hissed from its innards.

"Dessert," announced Sir Archibald.

Henry inhaled the symphony of sweet plums, pastry and red wine.

Viola licked her lips. They parted and wrapped around a luscious plum, skewered on the end of her dessert fork.

"She's a handsome woman, Doctor Collins." Lady Calthorpe whispered, barely audible above the murmur of table conversation and clatter of utensils.

Henry swallowed a mouthful of plum pie and opened his mouth to reply. Never had Lady Calthorpe been so direct.

Lady Calthorpe leaned closer.

"What are you going to do about it?" she asked.

Henry blinked and cleared his throat.

"Do?" he asked.

"Being a widow does offer one certain allowances but it has been almost three years," replied Lady Calthorpe as she glanced in Viola's direction. "She won't wait forever."

Henry regarded Viola.

"I envy you, Sir Archibald," she said. "I long to attend the World Fair."

"Paris is not that far," Sir Archibald replied.

Viola grinned and popped another plum into her mouth. She had the same spark when she first sped off on her plectocycle. Henry smiled.

"I admire Doctor Stewart's independence," he said quietly.

"It's one thing to be independent..." Lady Calthorpe picked up her fork. "But it's another thing to broadcast it so brashly." She stabbed at her dessert and scooped up a mouthful. "People are beginning to whisper."

Henry's moustache twitched. He watched Viola chase the last crumbs around her plate. She was happy.

Lady Calthorpe lowered her voice until it was barely audible.

"Gallivanting around London. In the middle of the night. With eligible bachelors... and no chaperone? Isn't exactly condoned by polite society, even for a widow of independent means," she said.

"What can I do?" asked Henry.

"If she were married...?"

His heart froze.

"What if she won't have me?" he asked.

Lady Calthorpe sighed and looked him in the eye.

"I've seen how she looks at you," she replied.

Henry shook his head. Surely Viola would choose freedom over marriage?

"If the whispers spread, what little independence Society has allowed her will be lost." She nudged a plum on her plate. "I do love our morning teas, hearing of her exploits. I don't want to lose that vicarious pleasure, Doctor Collins."

A gong reverberated through the room. Sir Archibald rose from his chair.

"Ladies, if you will excuse us, we have business to discuss. We'll meet you in the observatory in one hour. My man, Bothwell, will escort you when it's time. I'm sure you have much to discuss."

Henry rose from his chair and bowed. Lady Calthorpe smiled in his direction.

"Courage, Henry," he whispered to himself.

An earthy aroma filled the velvet-lined room. A fire crackled in the hearth. Henry leaned back into his snug over-stuffed armchair, sipped his port and observed his companions. Wisps of pipe smoke curled around Sir Archibald's head. He sipped on his pipe, pursed his lips and puffed. A perfect ring of smoke rose into the air, expanding as it rose above his head and dissipated along the ceiling. He offered Henry his tobacco tin.

Henry raised his hand and shook his head.

"You won't get him to indulge." Lord Calthorpe smiled. His mechanical hand trembled. He downed his port, placed his glass on the octagonal occasional table and retrieved a thin cigar. Acrid smoke pierced the swirling pipe smoke.

"Young Collins here says these may kill us," Lord Calthorpe chuckled.

"There are reports of heart paralysis," said Henry.

"Tosh. One confectioner, in 1863?" said Sir Archibald. He puffed his pipe in reply.

Henry smoothed his moustache. It wasn't often he had Sir Archibald on a hook, and he wasn't about to let him go.

"There was a recent report in the United States. It weakens the mental faculties and causes nervousness," replied Henry.

Lord Calthorpe coughed as he scowled at the cigar in his hand and stubbed it on a silver plate on the table beside him.

"Americans!" said Lord Calthorpe. "Must they always insist on spoiling an Englishman's enjoyment?" A metallic finger twitched. He filled his glass to the brim and quaffed the port in one gulp. His hand jittered. Lines etched deeper into his forehead. He rose from his chair and shoved his hand into a coat pocket.

"If you will excuse me, Sir Archibald." Lord Calthorpe bowed his head and turned to Henry. "My apologies, Doctor Collins."

The poor fellow. It must pain him to rely on a mechanical.

"No apologies required, Lord Calthorpe." Sir Archibald lowered his pipe and stood.

Henry rose from his over-stuffed armchair.

"No, no. You both continue." Lord Calthorpe raised his flesh hand. "I should probably get my wife home before this darned thing gets the better of me."

"Very well." Sir Archibald pressed a brass button on the wall, next to the dusty tapestry pull. "Bothwell will see you out."

All three nodded farewell in unison.

Henry picked up his glass and wandered over to the fireplace, twirled the glass in his fingers. The cut crystal sparkled in the firelight. The port glowed blood red.

"He's a braver man than I," he said.

Sir Archibald raised an eyebrow.

"Come on, Collins. His wife isn't that bad."

Henry's eyes widened. "No, I didn't mean–"

Sir Archibald chuckled.

Henry eyed his friend and swallowed his port. All these years and he still fell for Sir Archibald's verbal traps. He sighed and cleared his throat.

"What I meant was, I doubt I'd have the courage to have a mechanical implant." He raised his glass in Sir Archibald's direction. "Even if by England's most eminent biometric mechanical specialist, by Royal Appointment."

"Touché." Sir Archibald smiled, grasped the crystal carafe off the side table and joined Henry by the fire.

"Speaking of courage..." Sir Archibald placed the carafe on the mantelpiece and eyed Henry through slitted eyelids. "Have you asked her?"

Henry's eyes widened. His moustache twitched.

"Asked who, what?" he said.

"Henry, it's been three years. I see the way you look at her. Hell, everyone does." Sir Archibald placed his hand on Henry's shoulder. "How much longer are you going to torture yourself?"

Henry stared into the fire. The flames licked the charred log.

"She's happy, Archie," replied Henry. Flames danced in the air. Free. Like Viola. "She won't want to be burdened with another husband."

"Tosh!" Sir Archibald slapped Henry's back. "Gird your loins, man! What's the worst that could happen?"

The flames sputtered.

"What if she refuses me?" Henry whispered.

"She's your intellectual match, Henry. You need someone who will challenge you." Sir Archibald poured Henry another drink. "And she doesn't flinch when you arrive smelling of formaldehyde."

The flames flared and redoubled their efforts, their tongues licking the grate. Henry turned to his friend.

Sir Archibald topped up his glass and grinned.

"Stop brooding and get on with it," said Sir Archibald. "Viola's a handsome woman. If I were ten years younger..." He sipped his port. "If you wait too long, you'll miss out. Again."

Henry stared into the fire. His face burned. His stomach twisted. He clenched his free hand. Ten long years of waiting, watching his friend's happiness. Feeling guilty. Now he had his opportunity...

A quiet tap on the door caught their attention.

"Excuse me, gentlemen." Viola stood in the doorway, silhouetted by the hall light. Her hair shone like a halo around her face. "Lady Calthorpe sends her heartfelt regret she will not be able to attend the Mars Viewing."

"Do come in, Doctor Stewart," said Sir Archibald.

Viola took a step forward, toward the firelight, and hovered in the doorway.

"If you could order a carriage for me also?" She glanced at the smouldering cigar and bit her lip; it glistened in the firelight, red as the flames. "I don't want to intrude."

Viola's voice was sweet and rich, like the port. Henry's stomach clenched tighter. He couldn't bear it if he were to lose her again.

She gazed in Henry's direction. A smile flickered over her face. Henry straightened his shoulders, took another swig to fortify himself, and exhaled slowly, willing his muscles to relax.

"Nonsense. There's no need for you to leave." Sir Archibald flipped open his pocket watch. "We were just about to adjourn to the observatory. Mars waits for no one." He turned to Henry and winked. "Collins, be a good chap and escort Doctor Stewart to the observatory. I'd be a poor host if all my guests missed the main event." He turned to Viola. "I'm sure you remember how to work the telescope. The co-ordinates are set."

Viola nodded. Small creases formed at the corner of her eyes.

So very happy.

"Bothwell will show you up." Sir Archibald bowed low and left.

Henry and Viola were alone. She held out her hand in Henry's direction and wiggled her fingers.

"Come on, Henry. We don't want to be late."

Henry swigged his port.

No more excuses.

The compact observatory was twice as tall as it was wide. It faced south, away from the offending street lamps and bustle of London. A majestic tube of polished brass reached almost the full height of the two-storey room. A small tower, encircled by ornate iron stairs, supported the tube and a series of massive cogs sat above the wheels, ready to propel the contraption around a circular track buried in the tiled floor.

The gaslight dimmed.

The metal roof cover whirred and clunked. It inched open to reveal the night sky, and shuddered to a halt – like a huge slit iris - exposing a domed skeleton of metal struts and glass.

Henry looked skyward. Light glinted on the domed, multi-paned glass roof. Steam fizzled and hissed behind the sidewall. The glass dome slipped away. Stars twinkled in the heavens.

He stepped toward the telescope.

Viola skipped up the stairs and set to pulling levers.

Cogs ticked as they ratcheted the contraption's nose skyward. The tube moaned. The floor vibrated through the soles of his shoes. The telescope wobbled, and lurched, and hovered momentarily before beginning its slow, steady excursion.

Henry's moustache twitched. A smile flickered over his lips as Viola slid part way down the staircase and jumped off the bottom step. Her boots clicked as she landed on the tile floor.

"We're off to Mars." Her eye glinted in the dim light. She gathered her skirt train around her bustle, dodged the swinging telescope and slipped past Henry, brushing her back against Henry's arm in the confined room.

Henry's skin tingled. He caught his breath and glanced at Viola, hoping she had not heard him.

Viola positioned herself under the telescope, grasped the tube and peered into the eyepiece. She paced the room, keeping step with the telescope as it tracked the planets.

Click. Click.

Viola's gathered skirts accentuated the curve of her lower back and legs as she followed the telescope.

Click. Click.

A hint of red stocking flashed beneath the lifted hem.

Click. Click.

Henry's heart thumped keeping step with each footfall.

Click. Click. Click.

Viola glanced over her shoulder.

"Come and look, Henry. It's almost there."

Henry let his breath escape, slowly and silently, and joined her.

"See?" Viola pointed into the eyepiece.

Henry stooped slightly, searching the lens as he kept step with Viola. There was nothing but blackness.

The ratcheting stopped. The telescope shuddered to a halt. Viola paused mid-step. Henry collided into her; his chest pressed against her body. Her breath tickled the hair on his neck. Silk rustled as she released her skirts. His heart raced.

"My apologies," Henry pulled away. Had she felt his racing heart?

"Apology accepted." Her voice rolled over him like a warm spring breeze.

"I should see what's keeping Sir Archibald," whispered Henry. "He'll miss the main event."

Viola pointed at the eyepiece.

"Henry, you don't want to miss this." Fine lines caressed the corners of Viola's eye.

Henry stepped closer and dipped his head to see through the lens. A hazy, pink disc crept into one corner of the view.

"Is it supposed to be blurred?" he asked Viola.

"You need to focus." Viola's face brushed against his hair.

Henry stared down the lens, struggling to keep his breaths even.

The fuzzy disc continued across the lens.

He wanted to turn around, take her in his arms and feel her heartbeat racing, as his was.

What if it wasn't? What if he declared his intentions and was refused? His heart skipped. He would lose her.

Forever.

Henry swallowed. He raised one hand to the brass dial on the eyepiece and turned the dial away from him. The disc dissolved into the dark sky.

Things would never be the same. His heart sank.

Warmth embraced Henry's body, his arm. Fingers kissed his hand.

His skin tingled. The fingers hesitated, and curled around his fingers, gently edging the dial toward him.

Henry's heart somersaulted and lunged into his ribcage.

The pink disc solidified in the centre of the lens. Henry took a deep breath. He felt a soft rhythm beating on his back, through his jacket, through his waistcoat. His heart ricocheted in his chest. Each thump matched the beat of Viola's heart.

The dial turned again. The disc's edge cleared.

Henry held his breath, not daring to move. Not a muscle. Nothing that would break the spell.

They watched Mars traverse the lens, in silence.

Gears whirred. The telescope was about to move, to continue tracking the planet. The moment would be lost. Viola would be lost.

Breathe. Henry closed his eyes.

"Viola?"

"Yes, Henry?" Viola's hand remained.

The telescope shuddered.

Henry opened his eyes, turned his hand and slipped Viola's fingers between his. The pounding on his ribcage quickened. Was it his heart, or hers?

Now or never.

Cogs ratcheted. The telescope nudged to one side, leaving Henry and Viola behind. Henry clasped Viola's hand close to his chest and turned to face her. She stared at him - her pupil encircled by a sliver of iridescent green. So dark. He could feel his body falling.

Enough!

His arms encircled Viola's waist. Her fingers tightened. He could feel her body against his, her lips on his. He was losing control. And he didn't care.

Their lips parted.

"Viola?" Henry took a deep breath. "Will you marry me?"

Viola smiled.

"I thought you would never ask," she said.

THE END

Eye of the Beholder

Chapter 1:
Something Wicked This Way Comes

The grinding of the heavy double gate set Professor Fosse's teeth on edge. The iron bars rattled as it slammed shut, encasing them in gloom. Gone were the light-filled corridors and airy rooms laid out for public view. Gone were the tranquil chirps of the caged birds kept to pacify the more fortunate inmates. Far-off cries and screechings echoed through the empty hallway before them.

Keys chinked at the Warden's hip. They descended into the bowels of Bedlam, leaving the sane world behind them. The stench of sweat and urine burned his nostrils as he followed the Warden past ironbound doors. Hinges rattled.

The Warden paused. The way ahead was barred and locked.

Finger gears whirred inside Fosse's left glove. He pulled the leather tighter. His flesh hand trembled. He had not set foot in Bedlam since… His heart thumped. *How long had it been?* He took a slow breath, filling his lungs with the foul air.

Not long enough.

Now he faced the core of pandemonium again. He clenched his lean fingers and straightened his shoulders. It was louder than he remembered.

"Are you certain?" asked the Warden, as the key touched the lock.

Fosse closed his eyes and relaxed his fingers. He was a man of science, of facts. He sucked in the foul air, opened his eyes and nodded.

The Warden lit his lantern. The light sputtered. The rancid smell of tallow filled the corridor.

Beyond the portal lay rows of barred cells, each with its own cacophony of stenches. Fosse breathed through his mouth and stared at the back of the Warden's head. It bobbed along the corridor then turned and jerked toward one of the cells.

"That's him."

A wheezing lump of rags pressed into one corner.

Fosse studied the lump. The Lord Banbury he knew would roar objections, demand his release. This creature cowered in the shadows. *How could I have been so naive? No one remains untouched by twelve months in Bedlam.*

He swallowed. "Are you certain?"

"Dunno what he was once. Only what he is now," said the Warden.

"I need to speak with him. In private."

"He won't talk. Thinks he's being followed. We're all out to get him. Pretty much standard for here." The Warden knocked at the bars with his nightstick.

Banbury's eyes flickered in their direction.

Fosse leaned closer. "Lord Banbury?" He cleared his throat. "Hello. Remember me? Fosse? I need to ask you something. Something important."

Banbury's eyes widened - red and jaundiced. He scuttled to the bars. The gaunt face wedged between the metal. Lice crawled in the beard, somersaulting as the lips mumbled. Stale breath engulfed them. Fosse screwed up his nose and leaned away.

Memories of Bay Rum cologne, of sweat and rancid oil distracted him - pungent, overpowering, always heralding Banbury's return from a dig. Fosse loathed that smell. A wave of nausea washed over him. He now longed for the sickly aroma. *Anything to drown out the stench.*

"What did he say?" he asked.

"He's always rambling on about something. Shadows, curses. Or cats. Pfft."

Banbury lunged at the Warden, spitting out an unintelligible slur of words.

"Yes, yes. We know," grumbled the Warden.

"What was that? What did he say?"

The Warden rolled his eyes. "Beware the eye."

"Beware the eye?"

"He's got a thing about eyes. Careful now. Don't get too close, or he'll try to scratch out yours."

Fosse frowned. Lord Banbury was once a well-respected man of science. Egyptologist. Mentor. This poor creature wasn't the real man; the man who sponsored him. The man who mentored him. The man who forfeited his position at the Museum, the position he now held.

What could've sent you mad?

Fosse dropped four crowns into the Warden's hand. "See he gets new clothes. And a haircut." Another coin fell into the palm. "Good man."

The aroma of spices filled the air. Dark velvet curtains cloaked the windows.

Flickering candlelight illuminated rows of occupied, mismatched wooden chairs. Shadows licked the steps of the, as yet unlit, temporary dais and the curtain that concealed the promised spectacle.

Pools of light erupted as a dark-suited young man lit the candelabra around the hall.

Chairs squeaked on the polished floor. The crowd squirmed, stared into the blackness and murmured.

Viola prodded the padding of her chair - a dining chair apparently roped into service to make up numbers.

A candelabrum rattled against the dais. Light shivered across the steps. The young man leapt to its defence, apologising to a lady seated in the first row as he steadied the candles.

He skipped up the steps and circled the dais, taper in hand, and lit the footlights. Flames sputtered along the edge of the platform.

Metal scaffolding dominated the dais. Polished gears and brass pistons gleamed. Articulated rods reached down toward a large veiled box and disappeared under the drapery. Gold flecks glittered through the fine-gauzed linen.

Viola adjusted her eye patch and bit her lip. She turned to her companion.

"Henry! How exciting."

Henry patted her hand and smiled. "I thought you might be intrigued."

She gripped his hand. "Who wouldn't?"

She turned to the sarcophagus and licked her lips.

A real mummy!

"The mechanicals must have cost a fortune. The permits alone for such an ostentatious display would've cost several months' wages."

"They enjoy Royal favour," said Henry. "Mechanicals always help when trying to impress."

"Perhaps they need more patronage to pay off the spectacle?" whispered Viola.

She surveyed the sea of top hats, silk bonnets and perfect coiffures. Much of high society had responded to the invitation. Lady Calthorpe, always present at any notable function, sat a few rows in front. She fussed with her bag, glanced around and slipped on her spectacles.

A small group of scholarly-looking gentlemen stood near a candelabrum, engaged in intense debate. Sir Archibald Huntington-Smythe, Doctor and specialist in biometric mechanical technology, peered back through the crowd. He dipped his hat in her direction and smiled. Viola nodded back.

"Henry, Sir Archibald's here."

"Hardly surprising. He designed the mechanicals," replied Henry.

"It would seem everyone who's anyone is here tonight."

Clouds of steam hissed and puffed into the air and rolled along the ceiling.

The audience gasped.

More candles flickered to life behind the contraption, revealing a towering statue, half hawk-half man, staring back through the forest of candelabra.

The audience hushed.

Viola's eye widened and fixed on the veiled sarcophagus before them.

A lanky, beak-nosed gentleman emerged from behind one of the curtains on the dais. His hand slid along the crest of the sarcophagus, pausing to rest at the foot. He straightened his shoulders and beamed at the seated aristocracy, scientists and assembled society.

"Good evening, gentlemen." His voice boomed over their heads. "And ladies. My name is Mr Chartha, assistant to our esteemed head of Egyptian Antiquities, Professor Fosse." Chartha bowed low, not taking his eyes off his audience. He cleared his throat. "I'm afraid Professor Fosse has been unavoidably detained. However, the British Museum welcomes you. Tonight we celebrate our latest acquisition from the tombs of Egypt with the unwrapping of the mummy."

Another murmur rolled through the audience. Chartha raised his hands.

"Never fear, the unwrapping will continue on schedule and I will be able to answer any and all questions."

He clapped his hands together. "Now, shall we start?" His gaze flickered over the veiled sarcophagus entombed within the scaffold. "Here we have an untouched mummy from the nineteenth dynasty. The markings confirm it is a royal sarcophagus - a princess. Possibly a queen. Queen Mehytenweskhet?" He grinned at the audience as his tongue rolled effortlessly over the word. "So, we are anticipating some valuable treasures to be encased within the linen wrappings."

All you need now is a basket and a snake.

Chartha reached down beside the coffin and pulled a lever on the scaffolding. The contraption chugged into life.

The crowd gasped.

"Who among you is brave enough to join me in removing the initial wrappings?" Mr Chartha grabbed the edge of the linen and flicked it off the sarcophagus.

The woman, in the chair beside Viola, shrieked.

Viola winced and shook her head, her ears still ringing as the woman slumped. Her husband slipped his arm around her waist and fanned her furiously.

Viola rubbed her ear. *Such a commotion over nothing.*

Chartha pointed in their direction. "You, sir, would you like the honour?"

Viola gasped. *A chance to unwrap a mummy!*

Henry shook his head. A tinge of red crept along his earlobe.

"It seems the gentleman needs some encouragement. Mr Turner, would you escort the gentleman."

Viola smiled. "Go on, Henry. It sounds like fun."

Henry nudged Viola. He lifted her hand into the air, enticing her to her feet.

"But Henry, you–"

A familiar voice spoke by her ear. "Go on, Doctor Stewart," said Sir Archibald. "I unwrapped my first mummy at the London Museum. It's a curious thing, not unlike an autopsy."

Henry took her hand in his. "You go, Viola." He nudged her towards Turner, who now stood at the end of their row. "It'll give you something to tell Doyle next time you visit."

"Sir?" Turner held out his arm toward the dais.

"Go, Viola. Since when have you been so shy?" said Sir Archibald.

Viola pulled in her skirts and edged past Henry. A frown flickered over Turner's forehead.

The woman next to Viola roused. Her hands trembled. "But the curse…?"

Sir Archibald scoffed.

"Tish, there's no such thing as curses, dear lady," replied Henry.

"Hush, Henry." Viola winked at her fiancé and turned to the woman. She was as pale as a corpse. "Don't worry. A little curse won't stop me," she said.

Viola unhooked her purse from her arm and passed it to Henry. She was not about to let superstition rob her of such an exciting experience.

"Ah, yes?" Chartha was all smiles. "Miss…?"

"Doctor Stewart," replied Henry from his seat.

"A physician?" asked Chartha.

Sir Archibald stood. "Scientist," he replied.

"Excellent. Doctor Stewart, please join me," said Chartha.

A sea of candlelit faces turned toward her. Turner's frown slipped from his face. He nodded and ushered her to the sarcophagus.

The warm, honeyed smell of beeswax drifted around the candelabra as they approached the steps. Viola sniffed the air. Thick sweetness cloaked the dais.

More expense, but it'll mask the odour. How clever.

The sarcophagus was larger than expected. Deep carvings etched the edge of the coffin and extended down the centre of the lid. Remnants of jewel-coloured pigment covered the raised sections.

"Is this your first unwrapping, Doctor Stewart?" asked Chartha

Viola nodded.

"This is the inner sarcophagus. You can see part of the outer sarcophagus behind us." Chartha waved his hand in the direction of the large stone lid then at the markings on the inner sarcophagus, his dark eyes not leaving his audience.

"The oval panel is called a cartouche. The hieroglyphs inside it identify this as the final resting place of Princess Mehytenweskhet."

Viola examined the artwork: Deep azure, vermilion and rich golden yellow remnants of pigment clung to the wood. Flecks of gold leaf glittered through layers of ingrained dust. An ornate symbol of an eye, overlaid on the chest, obscured part of the cartouche. The sable paint glistened in the candlelight. *Not a trace of dust.*

Viola frowned.

She traced her hand along the outline of the symbol. Her glove tugged on the paint.

Still tacky. The paint was fresh. This was new; not part of the original markings.

Curious.

"First we need to break the seal. It can be difficult after all these-"

His voice buzzed in Viola's ear. Distracting. She leaned closer and squinted, scrutinising the lid, trying to see clearly in the flickering light.

The lid was out of alignment, not flush with the base. She placed her hands on the edge of the lid and pushed. It didn't budge.

The crowd gasped.

"You are keen, Doctor Stewart." Chartha's voice quietened to a more conversational tone.

Viola pointed to the lid. "The seal is already broken," she whispered.

Chartha's gaze flicked away from his audience to the sarcophagus. His jaw muscles pulsed.

They leaned forward, in unison, to examine the seal.

A lone voice squealed near the back. "Careful, the curse!"

There had been many outrageous accounts of mummies' curses and the disasters that befell the defilers of The Valley of the Kings. Enough stories to drive a crowd to hysteria.

All balderdash, of course.

Viola bit her lip, glanced across the lid and scanned the wide-eyed, white faces, pausing when she saw Henry. His moustache twitched. He winked and nodded. Dear, sweet Henry. Encouraging, as ever.

Viola breathed out slowly, feeling each muscle in her chest relax. She placed her hands on the sarcophagus lid and pushed. The wet paint pressed through her glove and dampened her fingers.

The lid remained unyielding.

Chartha harrumphed and cleared his throat.

"The miracle of modern mechanics meets the wonder of Ancient Egypt." His voice projected around the hall.

He pushed a lever on the mechanical contraption. Steam hissed from the base of the metal frame. Gears turned, knocking the pistons into life. The sarcophagus lid creaked and hissed as it separated from the coffin, rising an inch. Two inches. Three inches. The gears ground and slipped. The lid halted. The pistons froze. The lid shuddered.

Chartha cursed under his breath. He wrenched the lever back and motioned for help.

The smell of sickly sweet resin tickled Viola's nostrils. Whispers buzzed through her head. She shook her head and tugged her ear. Light flashed at the far end of the room. A door slammed.

"Turner!" Chartha rattled the lever.

Turner skipped up the steps, grabbed the dislodged corner of the coffin lid and wrenched it to one side. He grimaced and flicked his hand.

"Excuse me, Doctor." Chartha slipped in front of Viola and grasped the opposite corner of the lid.

The two men lifted it clear and propped it against the wall. Turner grabbed a candelabrum with both hands, walked it closer to the lid and adjusted it until gold reflections danced across the dais floor.

Dark smudges stained the candelabrum pole. Blood dripped from Turner's palm. He flicked open a handkerchief, from his top pocket, and wrapped his hand as he melted back into the shadows.

Puffs of steam percolated up from the contraption and crept over the sarcophagus. Chartha waved the vapours away, grumbled quietly, his thin lips frozen in a snake-oiled grin. He glared in the direction of Sir Archibald and, with a deep breath, he sighed, faced his audience and oozed charm once more.

He unfurled his arms wide, and with a final flourish of his wrists, bowed his head low.

"Presenting Princess Mehytenweskhet!" He raised an eyebrow. "Note the quality of the linen used to wrap the mummy." His fingers slid off the cream fabric. "Some of the finest I have encountered. We may indeed have a Queen."

Viola peeked over his shoulder into the sarcophagus. Loose-woven linen wrapped the body. Hemp cord tied the bundle snugly around the neck, legs and feet.

"Would you like the honour, Doctor Stewart?" Chartha produced a shiny, curved knife and presented it, handle first, to Viola. "Just slice down the middle of the chest..."

"Wouldn't unwinding it preserve the original wrappings and ensure the body isn't accidentally damaged?" asked Viola.

Chartha turned his face away from the crowd and spoke in low tones. "Yes, but we can access the treasures faster this way. We must give our patrons what they expect, and they expect a show."

Viola smiled and glanced toward Henry. He stood next to Sir Archibald. Both men smirked. They'd seen her skill with a blade. She would enjoy displaying her abilities before an audience.

I'll give you a show.

"Thank you, Mr Chartha."

Viola took the knife. It was not unlike an autopsy scalpel. She pierced the wrappings with the tip of the blade and, with a twist of her wrist, slipped it under the cords and the outer layer. The knife sliced easily through the outer layer of linen.

Another cry drifted up from the audience. Followed by a thump. A chair scraped. Soft footsteps tapped toward the back of the hall. Then silence. A faint murmur rolled through the gathering.

Chartha eyed Viola. "What sort of scientist are you?" he asked.

Viola smiled. "Optical," she replied. She offered him the knife. "And assistant to the Police Surgeon when the occasion arises."

Chartha's smile dropped. He licked his lips; the corners of his mouth quickly regained their composure. He motioned toward the sarcophagus.

"Shall we continue, Doctor Stewart?"

The wrappings peeled away cleanly, exposing a layer of criss-crossed fabric sheathing the body.

Chartha addressed the crowd. "Here were have the inner wrappings. Often trinkets of great value are found hidden amongst these layers, or on the mummy itself. It is thought such items were used to help ease one's path into the afterlife and–"

Viola plunged the knife into the chest area and sliced the wrappings along the sternum. The knife clinked against something solid inside the wrappings. Gold glinted through the opening.

"Ah, our first treasure!" announced Chartha.

"Shall I?" asked Viola as she placed the knife on the edge of the sarcophagus.

Chartha nodded. "You are entitled to first spoils."

Viola plucked up a corner of linen shroud and peeled it back from the body. She slipped her fingers into the cut and plucked out a small golden amulet. She held it up and examined it in the candlelight.

It was a falcon. Sapphire eyes glinted above the enamelled inlays decorating the wings.

Viola gasped. Her heart fluttered. This trinket had lain next to the heart of royalty for thousands of years. Now she held it in her hand. She pivoted the ornament to catch the light.

So beautiful...

"Well done, Doctor Stewart. Now shall we see if there are any other trinkets to share amongst the other guests?"

He pulled back more of the shroud, revealing the bound arms of the mummy, laid over the abdomen. Intricate folds of tight-woven linen wrapped the face, the hands, legs and feet. Deliberate, time-consuming work for the priests-embalmers.

"Correct me if I'm wrong, Mr Chartha," whispered Viola, "but don't royal mummies usually have their arms crossed over their chest?"

Chartha nodded.

"Oh, dear. The patrons will be disappointed," said Viola.

"Then I had better find more trinkets." He snatched up the knife, leaned in and cut into the wrappings.

The smell of putrefaction overpowered that of the sweet resin. Viola wrinkled her nose. The knife hung in the air, its tip quivering.

Chartha sniffed the body and coughed, slapping his hand over his mouth as he retched. "I suppose you are acclimated to foul stenches?"

The room shuddered. Chairs lurched, their occupants unaware as they gaped at Viola.

Flashes of light cracked around her, cracked out of the coffin, cracked inside Viola's head. Everything dimmed.

The buzzing swarmed around Viola.

She shook her head and sucked in a mouthful of air. Decay. Death.

She coughed. The hum reverberated through her skull.

A towering, angular figure loomed in the shadows behind the crowd. Its flaming eyes burned into her very soul.

Viola leaned on the rim of the sarcophagus to steady herself.

Footsteps rang on the steps beside them.

"Viola? Are you alright?" Henry's muffled voice droned in her ear.

Viola felt pressure around her waist. She clawed at the encumbrance. Henry flinched.

"What's wrong, Viola?" His voice was barely audible.

Viola blinked and squinted through the dimness. Chartha beside her, knife still in hand. Henry was on her other side. Her neck muscles relaxed; she collapsed into his embrace.

"I'm fine. Just a headache," she muttered.

"It's the mummy's curse!"

Through the blurred haze, a pale figure rose from beside the shrieking woman in the front row. It wavered. A shadow joined it. They stumbled from the room, into the thickening fog beyond.

"The sight of a mummy can be disturbing to the fairer sex." Chartha's voice boomed through the hum.

Viola wanted to crack him over the head. If only her legs hadn't betrayed her.

"I don't think -" Henry began.

Viola pulled herself upright. She turned to their host. "I'll wager I've seen more dead bodies than you."

Henry chuckled. "I'd take that wager."

"Sir?" Chartha spoke through gritted teeth. "And you are?"

"Doctor Henry Collins. Marylebone Police Surgeon."

"Ah." Chartha cleared his throat. "Shall we proceed?"

"A good suggestion."

Viola focused on the inner coffin. Shapes coalesced. Henry loosened his hold on her waist as he leaned over the mummy.

"It's supposed to smell like that?" he asked.

"No." Chartha stumbled backward, his face an ashen shade of green. "Musty. It is usually musty. Perfumed with–" He gasped. "With resin and oils."

Another door slammed. Sir Archibald called for calm.

Viola snatched the knife from Chartha's hand, slid it under the bandages and sliced open the shroud across the chest. Henry leaned forward and peeled the bandages free from the body.

The pungent smell of death leaked from the bundle and rose to meet them. Chartha recoiled further back as if hit by a rogue carriage. He spluttered into his hand.

The crowd erupted into whimpers and shouts.

Viola peered under the bandages, still clutching the amulet. Grey tweed covered the exposed chest. Waistcoat buttons pulled flush against the material, tugging it taut.

"Henry…" Viola touched Henry's arm.

She gently pressed the body with her free hand. The head jerked. The corpse groaned. The stench rumbled.

Next comes the–

A scream. A collapse in the front row.

Chartha coughed and heaved behind them.

Poor fellow.

A loud clattering filled the Lecture Hall. Men shouted. Muffled screams trailed from the room.

"I think we had better alert the Station," said Henry.

Daylight streamed through the skylight and glared off the metal autopsy slab. Viola's boots clicked on the tiled floor as she circled the table, a bundle of grey clothes in her arms. Henry hummed as he worked. His moustache wiggled rhythmically with the lively tune. Viola closed her eyes and drank in the notes; the humming warmed the silence of the room. She laid out the suit and examined the grey material - trousers, jacket, waistcoat.

A grey suit? Just need a grey bowler and...

Viola ran her hand over the waistcoat. Small tufts of loose thread tickled her finger as she scratched at a small hole in the weave.

"Something has been ripped off the left side of the waistcoat, Henry."

She recorded the finding in her notebook, wrapped the suit in a labelled brown paper package and tied it off with string. Something wasn't right. Something she couldn't quite...

Viola frowned and pushed the package across the bench next to the pile of linen wrappings. Notebook in hand, she returned to Henry's side.

Henry placed a small mirror under the corpse's nostrils and examined it. Nothing. He pulled a wooden tube from a drawer under one of the side benches, placed the fluted end against the corpse's chest and listened.

"Surely he's dead," Viola held her breath.

Henry went quiet and raised an eyebrow.

The stench of decay filled the room. Viola grimaced. It was a silly question.

"Procedures must be followed," replied Henry. "We don't want him waking up to find his entrails lying over our table."

"That would be unfortunate," Viola rolled her eyes.

"Negative life signs."

Viola sighed silently, scribbled down the results and returned the notebook to the side bench. The echo of her boots, as she returned to the table, reminded her of the clapping audience in the Lecture Hall, the figure looming in the shadows... His eyes. Hairs raised on her arm.

The wooden tube clattered on the bench. Henry hummed a calming tune.

Viola swallowed and examined the body. Pale red, sharp-edged blemishes covered the chest. Henry crouched low, his head level with the table. Viola leaned over and peered along the epidermis of the torso.

Flat. No trace of disturbance. These marks are post mortem.

Henry swabbed the dried blood from the body; water bled from the sponge onto the table and dribbled off into a metal bowl.

"There's a scratch on the chest, over the heart area," he said. "That would match the damage on the waistcoat."

Viola placed a hand on the torso and frowned. "It's still warm." *Just like Cheops in Mrs Loudon's book.*

"Perhaps he is cursed?" Viola bit her lip.

Henry wangled the dripping sponge in Viola's direction.

"Nothing supernatural about it. I don't believe that twaddle."

Henry's moustache twitched. Viola caught a flicker of a frown as he eyed the bundles on the bench. He turned to her and smiled.

"Perhaps the linen wrappings and close confines insulated the body?" he said, with a wink. Viola licked her lips. How could she explain the shadowed figure she'd seen in the Lecture Hall?

An hallucination? But, that would mean... She swallowed. *No, better to be cursed than mad.*

"Of course." She swallowed. *I'm not mad!*

Henry lifted one of the body's arms and flexed the finger joints.

"No rigor mortis."

He rolled the body on to its side. Large red-blue patches covered the back, buttocks and right leg. Viola peered at the corpse.

"The markings are only on one side," said Viola, "He was placed in the coffin *after* he was dead?"

Henry glanced up at Viola and nodded. "It would appear so."

"And the body insulated to conceal the time of death?"

Henry nodded and crooked his head.

"It does complicate things." He retrieved the sponge. "There could be significant head trauma." He dipped the sponge into a bowl of water and squeezed it tight. Pink drops of water plopped back into the bowl. "Pass me the bone saw, Viola. Let's get a look inside the skull."

Henry hummed a sweet tune as he dragged the sponge across the forehead, removing clots from the ginger locks.

The tune died mid-note.

He peered at the skin, frowned and wiped gently at the scalp.

"No need for the saw," he said.

Henry clasped the head in his hands. The scalp twisted with a squelch. "I'll need the chisel."

The saw clattered onto the table. Viola wrinkled her nose as she passed the chisel.

There was a sickening, sucking sound as Henry peeled off the cranial cap. The brain jiggled. The two halves slowly separated. Viola lunged her hands forward, grasped the collapsing organ to prevent it from falling. It squelched in her hands.

"Someone's been here before us," said Henry.

Viola rolled her eyes.

Henry selected a scalpel and prodded at the exposed Corpus Callosum. Viola remained still, holding the two halves steady.

"Curious." Henry pressed his fingers into the pea-sized void. "The pineal gland has been removed."

The patter of Viola's footsteps ricocheted off marble columns that towered around the entrance hall of the British Museum. Henry's cane provided a counterpoint to the rhythm.

Tap. Tap. Tap.

Faint ticks and clacks drifted in from the courtyard and wove themselves into the beat.

A party of Toffs in top hats and silk-gloved ladies flocked down the grand staircase. The rhythm was lost in the uneven flurry of well-heeled footsteps.

Shadows followed them - flitted over the columns framing the staircase and crept across the marble steps toward Viola. She shuddered and glanced around the entrance hall, searching for a distraction, anything to focus on. Her head swam.

Anything but the shadows.

She spun on her heel, to be confronted by an enormous Italianate vase dominating the foyer.

Naked figures, festooned with over-sized clusters of grapes, frolicked around its edges in a Bacchanalian orgy. Fine lines of repaired cracks traced around the raised figures. Carved torsos erupted from the lower third of the vase and transformed into muscular feline limbs to support the vase on its pedestal.

Henry placed a soft hand on her shoulder and cleared his throat.

"Viola, this is no time to lollygag," he whispered. "You can enjoy the sights later. We have a meeting with Professor Fosse."

Viola nodded and glanced past Henry. Behind him stood the elegant party, their feet still. A perfectly primped debutante flicked her attention from Viola's eyepatch toward the vase. A faint smile peeked through her gloved fingers.

Viola followed the woman's gaze to the sculptured male figures on the vase. Naked men. Her cheeks burned.

Henry leaned closer. "Come, Viola. The Professor will be waiting. You can ask him about the eye symbol painted on the coffin lid."

"And the mummy's curse," said Viola.

Henry smiled.

"He's just returned from Edinburgh. Some family trouble, apparently."

Edinburgh? Viola pursed her lips. It was the last place she had seen– Her heart jumped.

Anne.

It had been several months since she had thought of her sister. A year since she had last gone searching. And months more since...

Viola's heart thumped, pushing hard against her lungs. She twisted the engagement ring on her left hand.

I've been too preoccupied with everything since Henry's proposal.

Her heart inched higher, nudging her throat. She swallowed.

I've been so selfish.

Henry frowned.

"Is everything all right, Viola?" he asked.

Viola let go of the ring, caught her breath and forced a smile.

"Of course," she replied.

A shadow flashed over the marbled floor in front of them.

Viola shivered. The shadowy vision in the Lecture Hall doorway still haunted her dreams. It still whispered to her, whispered her name...

Viola straightened her shoulders.

Henry slipped his arm around her elbow and escorted her toward the East Wing.

A tall, dark-suited young man hovered near the statues by the Eastern doorway. *There was something familiar...* He stepped into the sunlight and crossed the hall toward them.

"Doctor Collins and Doctor Stewart, I presume?" He extended a bandaged hand to Henry.

"And you are?" asked Henry.

"It's Mr Turner, isn't it?" replied Viola.

Henry raised an eyebrow. "You know this man?"

"Mr Turner assisted Mr Chartha at the Mummy Unwrapping."

"Assistant to Professor Fosse." Turner nodded.

"We were expecting Professor Fosse." Henry's moustache twitched. Turner dropped his hand.

"The Professor has been detained. He sent me to fetch you. Follow me, please."

Viola's eye widened. The Professor was either extremely busy or in serious need of a lesson in etiquette.

Turner turned and strode toward the East Wing.

Viola and Henry followed him through the Manuscript Department into the Royal Library; its inlaid wooden floors and coffered ceilings stretched almost the entire length of the quadrangle. Glass-fronted bookshelves, crammed with tomes, clung to the walls and reached up to the window-studded mezzanine.

Viola examined the display cabinets and polished tables as they passed. Elaborately calligraphed tomes and illuminated scripts glinted in their prisons. Their brilliant hues lured her closer.

Extraordinary.

"Do keep up," grumbled Turner as he strode on.

Embellished brass filigree and fine, wrought iron latticework patterned the glass cage of the Ascension Chamber. It was more attractive than the last such conveyance Viola had experienced. Viola took a deep breath. *That didn't end well.*

The British Museum was a showcase of the written word, specimens and artefacts of antiquity, but it was also the bastion of science; a new-fangled ascension chamber shouldn't have been unexpected.

Viola eyed the Ascension Chamber. *But still daunting.*

"Is this your first time in an Ascension Chamber, Doctor Stewart?" asked Turner as he stepped into the enclosure.

Viola nodded, gripped the iron rim of the concertinaed-door and bit her lip.

"There's no need for concern. It is perfectly safe," said Turner.

"I'm sure the maintenance is impeccable, Mr Turner." Henry proffered his hand to Viola, and smiled.

Blood thudded in her ears, as if to shout warning. She took his hand, pulled her bustle skirts clear of the door with her free hand, and closed her eye. Henry gently squeezed her hand as she stepped over the threshold. A reassuring warmth tingled through her fingers. The blood quietened.

Once inside, Viola opened her eye and scanned the chamber. It was an impressive design: parquetry floor, walls of ruby and lapis-coloured stained glass. The designs echoed the lines of the filigree, befitting the Royal presence.

Henry and Turner stood more than an arm's length away, sufficient room for the Queen's crinolined skirts while still allowing room for her personage to remain untouched. Silk rustled as Viola patted the folds of her draped skirts back in place.

Quite roomy with the fashionable narrower silhouette.

"Her Majesty donated both Ascension Chambers to the Museum. The Formal Ascension Chamber is in the south quadrangle, near the entrance hall," said Turner. "It's for the exclusive use of Her Majesty. This is Her Auxiliary Ascension Chamber, for the exclusive use of special guests, visiting dignitaries." The door rattled as he pulled it closed. "And the Queen herself, of course."

"We are honoured," replied Henry.

Turner pushed up a lever embedded into a decorated iron box on the side of the chamber. The cage trembled and lifted away from the ground. Viola's grip tightened on Henry's hand. He ran his thumb over her fingers.

Remain calm.

Elaborately inked papyrus documents decorated the walls of the chamber's shaft, their colours undiminished as they scrolled past the chamber's glass casements.

The light dimmed as they rose from the ground level.

Viola sucked in a short breath. Henry placed his other hand on hers. His fingers traced gently over her wrist. A warm calm flowed along her arm and cradled her heart. The thumping in her veins slowed.

Dear Henry.

Sunlight spilled through the east windows and into the cage as the Ascension Chamber emerged through the ceiling to the first floor. Shadows slithered across the parquetry floor.

Turner cranked a wheel next to the lever. The door opened, folding back on itself. Viola glanced up at her fiancé. The edges of his moustache lifted as he smiled. She let out a long, controlled breath and stepped out onto solid, unmoving ground.

Turner led them through another room, past massive sculptured slabs of men battling centaurs and warrior women.

"The Nineveh Gallery," announced Turner.

Voices droned, echoing through the unpopulated room. Long shadows crawled across the floor as they walked through the exhibits into the adjoining gallery.

Viola's heart raced. Her muscles twitched. This was childish, of course. To be frightened by shadows.

Just breathe. Slow. Calm.

The droning grew louder. Another shadow flitted past the doorway ahead.

Turner was gone. They were alone.

Viola flinched. She hesitated.

"Viola, can I help?" Furrows etched into Henry's forehead. "Perhaps we should reschedule our appointment?"

A ragged breath escaped. Viola dragged her attention from the doorway. The voices drew closer.

"Henry, I–"

A group of chattering women strolled from behind one of the large angular columns and congregated at the foot of a monumental sculpture of a winged lion. It stared down at them with blank eyes. A smartly dressed woman motioned toward the statue.

"Here we have an Assyrian relief sculpture thought to be that of Ashurnasirpal the Second..." The voice echoed around them.

"Viola...?" Henry raised an eyebrow.

"It's nothing, Henry."

Turner slid into view, just beyond the roving lecture group.

"Do keep up, Doctors," he said. He turned on his heel and strode ahead.

Henry escorted Viola onward.

Curiosity Cabinets huddled together along the entire length of the Egyptian Room gallery. All manner of trinkets, sculptures and personal items were stuffed in display cases along the walls. Linen-wrapped entities lay entombed in the glass coffins, under the watchful eye of jewel-coloured murals. Patches of golden lamp light bathed the ceiling, outshining the last rays of dying sunlight from the skylights and windows.

Viola took a deep breath. The musty smell of old cupboards, a hint of spices and the heady perfume of Frankincense filled the air.

A muffled mutter originated somewhere amongst the cabinets at the other end of the gallery, and was cut short by the clack of Viola's boot heels on the polished floor.

Other footsteps echoed through the gallery.

Viola halted. Her heart thumped as she scanned the exhibits.

The muttering silenced.

A wiry man in a tailored linen suit emerged from the cabinet racks near the far doorway. He folded up a wad of papers, shoved them inside his jacket, and straightened his cuffs. He peered along the aisle, pushed up his spectacles and strode towards Viola and Henry.

"Professor Fosse?" asked Henry.

Fosse squinted in Henry's direction and scowled.

"Yes, Mr...?" he asked.

"Doctor Collins, and–" Henry held out his right hand.

"Ah, this must be Doctor Stewart." Fosse bowed his head slightly, and eyed Viola's eye patch. Fosse's pupils consumed almost the entirety of each iris. The rims quivered as he sidestepped around her and turned his back to the windows, not taking his eyes from her.

Henry withdrew his hand and let it fall by his side.

Viola's fingers twitched. She curled them into her fist, fighting the urge to adjust her patch. Fosse's gaze lingered. She stared back. He definitely needed a lesson in etiquette.

Fosse cleared his throat.

"Just admiring the colour of your ensemble, Doctor Stewart. Did you know Lapis Lazuli was a favourite of the Pharaohs and their queens?" he asked.

A whirring of cogs emanated from his gloved left hand. He winced, clenched his fingers. Circular ridges formed where the glove tightened on the knuckles.

Henry proffered his card to Fosse.

"We are in need of your expertise, Professor Fosse," said Henry.

Fosse regarded the card and glanced up at Henry and Viola. His gaze lingered again on the eye patch.

"Police surgeon?" Fosse licked his lips and flicked the card. "I have already answered the Constabulary's questions." He slipped Henry's calling card into his breast pocket. He tapped it and smiled; the corners of his mouth barely moved.

"But you haven't answered ours, Professor," replied Viola.

Fosse raised an eyebrow. "And why should I, *Miss* Stewart?"

Viola's fingernails pressed deeper into her palm, as she searched for a polite response.

"*Doctor* Stewart is assisting me with my enquiries," said Henry. "We are trying to identify the deceased." Henry reached into his inside coat pocket and pulled out a photograph. Clouded eyes stared out from a pale face, framed with matted, red hair. "Is he known to you?"

Fosse blinked slowly and returned the photo to Henry.

"Sorry, he's not a friend of mine," he replied.

Viola regarded Fosse. *Carefully worded.* What's he hiding?

"It is strange you didn't attend the unwrapping, Professor Fosse," she said. "It must have been important business indeed to keep you from presenting your most significant find to your peers?"

Fosse met Viola's gaze. His eyelids stiffened.

"Private family matters, Doctor Stewart. I'm sure you understand."

Anne. Viola's heart pounded. *Does he know?* She took a deep breath. *If only I'd known...* Pain needled her gut.

I would've warned you about the monster. The monster who... Viola held her breath... *provided the only clue to your fate. I promised I would find you. I promise...*

She fiddled with the eye patch over her right socket.

Smooth, silk. She breathed slowly. Evenly. *How could I forget you, Anne?*

Viola tugged her gloves snug on each hand before she answered: "I understand."

One corner of Fosse's mouth curled.

Viola's muscles tensed. She wanted to run. To hide. *But why? What have I done?* She took a measured breath; she had survived worse bullying at university. *They too had resorted to personal attacks when all else failed.*

Henry's eyes flicked in her direction. Wrinkles nudged the corners.

Dear Henry. Viola returned a feeble smile. *No, Fosse was a coward.* She straightened her shoulders. *And one never gives into cowards.* She looked Fosse in the eye.

"There was an eye. A decorative eye, with a curved line from the bottom. Is that significant?" she said calmly.

Fosse tensed. Fingers clicked. Pupils wavered but remained dilated. He smiled with closed lips, his dark eyes remaining inanimate. He turned away.

"Follow me." He led Viola and Henry through a side door to his office. An assortment of Egyptalia - small statues and artefacts -

occupied the desk. A stack of journals perched on one corner, next to a fixed rectangular box with a prominent brass pushbutton. Behind the desk was a small library of books and journals, framed in mahogany.

Fosse's gloved fist ticked. He wiggled the fingers.

"This will have to be quick. I have another appointment."

Click. Click.

With his un-gloved hand, he pushed down the brass button on the box, leaned over the desk and pulled out a dog-eared tome.

He flipped through the pages.

Click.

"The Eye of Horus is a common funerary motif, a token of healing and restoration of life. Ah, here it is." He pressed his finger on the page. "The Eye of Horus is also known as the 'Wadjet' or 'all seeing eye'. Note the blue iris." Fosse's hollow gaze flicked in Viola's direction, and back to the book.

"It's a symbol of the sky god, Horus; often depicted as a falcon." He turned the page and scanned the text with his finger. "An ancient myth tells how Horus lost his left eye, during a battle with the god Set. The eye was magically restored by Thoth, hence is often a symbol of protection and healing. Eye amulets are often found within the linen wrappings, or as inscriptions on the coffin to aid in the afterlife."

Fosse turned another page.

"It was even used as a notation of measurement, divided into six parts. Each piece was–"

"But the symbol was freshly painted." Viola interrupted. *And why would someone do that? Who would do that?*

Fosse slapped the book shut.

"You can borrow my copy. It should provide any other answers you require."

His gloved hand chittered as he handed the volume to Viola.

Is his hand shaking?

"Thank you, Professor," she said.

Fosse clenched the hand and swallowed.

"I must get back to work. This unfortunate affair has disrupted the installation of my new collection." He ushered them to the door, paused, and spun on his heel to face them. "I shall have to send you an invitation to the Exhibit opening - to make up for the disappointment of the other night."

"That would be splendid," said Henry.

"Do you have a card, Doctor Stewart? So I can forward it to you?"

Viola presented him with her card.

Viola Stewart

OPTICIAN

Spectacles to Order

Manufacturer of optical instruments

"You work with eyes?" asked Fosse. He flipped the card. "Ah, Greater Marylebone Street. I shall have Turner organise an invitation at once."

"Yes, sir." Turner stood in the doorway holding a silver tea tray. A heady floral aroma wafted upward as Turner passed them and placed the tray on the desk.

With a hint of... Something bitter? The scent was vaguely familiar. *Something sweet? Rose?* Viola wrinkled her nose. She couldn't place the smell.

"I'll have Turner see you out," said Fosse.

"No need, my good man." Henry slipped his arm around Viola's elbow.

"I insist." Fosse plopped into his chair. "You will need him to operate the Ascension Chamber." He poured his tea, wrapped his hands around the cup and inhaled the aroma.

The sun angled low through the windows. Long shadows crept across the floor of the Egypt Room. Turner led Viola and Henry back through the Nineveh Gallery. Pools of light reflected off the glass walls of the Ascension Chamber. The alcove windows dimmed in the setting light.

Viola gulped a short breath and followed Turner into the enclosure.

Turner cranked the Ascension Room lever. The glass cage quivered and slowly descended.

Viola shifted her feet. Her skirts swished. She felt like a bluebird caught inside a brass cage. She concentrated on her breath.

Slower.

She stared through the filigreed walls to the open alcove beyond. To freedom.

A long shadow emerged and edged closer to the Chamber. A silhouetted figure glided into the doorway, merging with the shadow.

Viola flinched.

Trapped!

She glanced at the other occupants. Henry flipped open his pocket watch and tapped the crystal cover. Turner stared out in the direction of the windows.

I'm cowering at shadows again.

She returned her attention to the doorway, barely visible under the receding Chamber ceiling. The last ray of roof lighting reached toward the figure. It turned toward her. Red glinted at its throat.

The Chamber continued downward, wiping the vision from sight.

Just my imagination.

The basket creaked as the balloon climbed higher.

Air rushed over her face. It tugged at her loose hair and flung auburn tendrils across her eyes and into her mouth. Water rushed below them.

Knock.

The balloon sped forward, even closer to–

Viola held her breath.
Knock, knock.

...the Mummy.

Viola slipped her feet off the couch and glanced up from her book. Polly bobbed in the open doorway.

"Excuse me, Miss. A Mrs Edgar Fosse is here to see you."

"Mrs...?" Viola closed her book and placed it on the occasional table beside the couch.

"Fosse, Miss. She says you met her husband yesterday at the British Museum." Polly presented Viola with a crisp white calling card. The writing was uncluttered, professional. Just a name:

Mrs Edgar Fosse.

Viola straightened her bustle and neatened the voluminous folds of her skirts, brushing out the creases and straightening the pleats. She primped her hair and nodded.

"I'll bring some tea and cake before I leave," said Polly.

"You won't be late?" asked Viola.

Polly shook her head.

"Then, yes. That would be lovely." Viola adjusted her lace-edged eye patch. "Show Mrs Fosse in."

Beatrice Fosse swirled through the door. Her French gown glowed scarlet in the afternoon light. Yards of Chinese silk swished as she bustled across the room. A large carpet bag dangled from her arm, swaying in time to her footsteps. A heady, floral scent, with a hint of geranium, lingered in her wake.

Her gaze flickered over Viola's eye patch and darted to the book on the table.

"Mrs Fosse, to what do I owe the pleasure?" Viola rose to meet her guest.

"Please call me Beatrice, and do sit down." She plopped onto the overstuffed chair next to the couch. Her hair was tinged with grey, marking her as a woman of more years than her attire admitted. The perfume settled in a cloud around her.

"And I shall call you Viola." Beatrice took a quick breath and settled her black eyes on Viola's hand. "My, what a lovely ring." She lifted Viola's hand and rolled it this way, then the other. "I was told congratulations were in order. I believe Doctor Collins is the lucky man? Don't leave it too long before you set a date. You know what Doctors are like."

Viola felt her cheeks warm slightly. She shook her head and smiled politely.

"Now," Beatrice huffed. "I've come to offer the most sincere apologies for my husband's rude behaviour at the Museum, yesterday."

Viola bit her tongue. Beatrice was what her mother would've called polished brass. *No wonder the Professor was so terse. Perhaps he was not accustomed to verbal restraint, being bombarded by such endless prattling?*

"There's no need. I understand he's been under a great deal of pressure lately. The prize of his collection stolen? A murdered stranger? Indeed! I would be a little tetchy, too."

Beatrice clapped her hands together and leaned closer. "Oh, we are going to be grand friends!"

Viola bit her lip.

The teacups rattled on the tray as Polly entered the parlour. She lifted Viola's book from the edge of the occasional table, slipped the tea tray in place, and stacked the book on a haphazard pile of novels on a side table.

"I'll be back in time for afternoon tea, Miss," said Polly.

"Thank you, Polly. I hope your sister is feeling better soon," said Viola.

A quivering smile fluttered over Polly's lips. The door clicked shut behind her.

"How unfortunate," said Beatrice. "It's so hard to get good staff these days. It can cause chaos when they require time off." She cradled her bag in her lap. "Do you allow her much time off?"

"Just a few hours, two afternoons a week. It has no significant impact on the household, so I can't see any harm in it."

"She is very lucky to have a position with such a generous employer." Beatrice surveyed Viola's bookshelves.

"You have a fine selection of books, Viola." Her gaze slid over the side table. Her eyes widened.

"Is that a copy of *The Mummy*?" she asked.

"Yes." Viola raised an eyebrow. *So many questions. It was a wonder I get a word in.*

"Oh, I haven't read that yet. I do adore Mrs Loudon. Such a forward thinker." She poured herself a cup of Darjeeling. "Have you read her gardening books?"

"No, I–" replied Viola.

"I'll lend you one of mine." Beatrice beamed.

Viola shook her head. "Thank you, but–"

"The Mummy..." Beatrice peered at the book on the side table. "That does sound exciting."

"Would you like to borrow my copy?" she asked, as she reached for the teapot.

"That would be wonderful." Beatrice slipped her fingers around the pot handle and smiled. "Let me pour, Viola."

"Thank you. I'll get the first volume." Viola rose from the couch and crossed to the bookshelf.

"Sugar?" asked Beatrice.

"Two, please." A spoon clacked on china, behind her. Viola winced. *My best china.*

Viola fingered the spines of the books. *Volume three, volume... One.* She pulled out the book, returned to the couch and presented it to Beatrice.

Beatrice placed the book on her empty lap.

Viola sipped her tea under the watchful eye of her guest.

She sniffed the steam as it wafted passed her nostrils. *Flowers?* She sniffed again, slowly, letting the aroma work its way to her olfactory brain. It smelled of...

Beatrice. Beatrice and her all-pervading perfume.

The hot liquid swirled around the cup, tickling her lip. It was sickly sweet.

"Have some cake. Polly is famous for her fruitcake." Viola licked her lips. *How many sugars had Beatrice put in?*

"See, we are friends already." Beatrice nibbled on a piece of cake and swallowed. "My dear Viola." She leaned closer to Viola. "I have something I need to tell someone. You're medically trained. I am sure you'll understand." She balanced the fruitcake on the edge of her saucer and clasped her hands together. "I'm concerned about my husband. He's becoming unhinged. You see, his twin brother died and he's to take over the family's interests. I'm not sure if he can cope."

Finance was a subject more appropriate for her accountant, or at least close friends. Viola swallowed another mouthful of tea.

"I'm confident the Professor would do an admirable job. After all, he has experience managing large expeditions for the Museum," replied Viola.

Beatrice lowered her voice to a whisper. "He's consulted a spiritualist."

Viola's eyes widened. "Surely not? He is a man of science." *Though that had not daunted Arthur from dabbling in the occult.*

Viola cleared her throat. It was dry. She sipped her tea.

"Oh, yes. He has been researching into something called the Mind's Eye. He says it is the heart of the soul. He's almost fanatical about it." Beatrice frowned. "He goes on about how the dead stay with us. They try to influence us, and that we must protect ourselves from their curse." She fidgeted at the corner of Viola's book.

The sun flared across Viola's vision. She squinted and rose from her chair. "Do you mind if I close the curtains?"

"Not at all." Beatrice smiled at Viola as she crossed the room.

The curtains clattered mostly shut. A sliver of biting light bounced off a curio cabinet glass door.

"May I tell you something in confidence, Viola?"

What else could you say?

Beatrice leaned toward Viola. Her voice dropped to a whisper.

"Edgar's uncle ended up at Bedlam. He refuses to see him. I am forbidden to mention his name."

"Mrs Fosse, I–"

"Beatrice, please call me Beatrice." She leaned even closer, the book almost consumed by the folds of her skirt.

Viola's cheeks flushed. She wiped her forehead.

I must have a word to Polly about the heating.

Viola slid back into the couch. Beatrice's blurred face loomed before her.

"Beatrice, maybe you shouldn't share such confidences? Surely your husband–"

"Yes, yes. You're correct. Please don't tell him I confided in you or he will be very angry with me."

"Of course not," replied Viola. "It was in confidence." Her tongue almost tripped over the words.

"And you must promise not to tell Doctor Collins. I could not bear it if Edgar was sent to Bedlam as well."

"Bedlam? Why–?"

"He does get so agitated, but I could not bear to be alone." Beatrice's voice was foggy. "I am sure it is nothing serious." She grinned and tapped the teapot. "Would you like more tea?"

Viola licked her dry lips and nodded. She blinked, trying to focus on the cup. She guzzled the liquid down to quench her thirst. Her heart raced.

Another wave of heat rolled over her. The room darkened, blurred. A faint buzzing noise tugged at her consciousness.

Not again.

Light danced around her. Viola squinted, trying to quell the piercing pain in her eye.

Beatrice clutched Viola's book to her chest. The gilt words glared into Viola's face. She struggled to focus on the words written on the cover:

The Mummy!

Viola struggled to concentrate on the words echoing through the fog: "... and the sarcophagus. Surely, you must have been scared of the curse?"

"Curse?" slurred Viola.

"Don't all mummies inflict a curse if you open their coffins?" Beatrice lowered her voice to mimic that of her husband: "Whosoever shall disturb my sleeping place, shall die a horrible death…" She smiled and continued in her own voice: "Or something like that. Edgar made one of the hired men open the last one." She giggled.

"Oh, I almost forgot." Beatrice rummaged in her bag and pulled out a gilt-edged invitation. She plopped it on the table. The teapot rattled on the tray.

Viola reached out to steady the pot. Her fingers clutched at the air.

"Are you unwell?" Beatrice's voice was faint, a mere murmur.

A shadowy figure filled the doorway, outlined with a faint glow. It shuffled towards them, each limb dragging on the carpet. A swirling, grey fog crept closer with each step.

The bright edges coalesced, elongated and wrapped around its torso like loose linen bandages.

The figure groaned, reached toward Viola and tilted its head. The wrappings loosened and fell away from its face.

Viola gasped.

Anne! Anne, you've come back. She twisted towards the apparition; her elbow slipped off the arm of the couch.

Anne opened her mouth. Viola strained to hear the words.

Silence.

A door slammed.

The buzzing circled them, swarming over Anne, dragged her to the ground, dragged her into an erupting mound of earth. She clawed at the earth, as she sank deeper, until only her linen-wrapped fingers were visible.

Then she was gone.

The click of the library door silenced the buzzing.

The room filled with scuffles, more murmurs. Wailing.

Shadows floated off the chair and drifted out of the room.

Another bang.

Polly's face emerged from the fog.

"Miss?" A sharp stinging pain dashed across her face. "Doctor Stewart!"

Another wave of heat enveloped her body.

"I'll fetch Doctor Collins."

Polly's face melted into the shadows. The curtain cords hissed. The edge of the couch slipped away.

The gilt lettering danced above the covers of her book, left on the empty chair beside her. The book wriggled and flopped to the floor. A linen wrapped hand rose from the depths of the carpet and wrapped its fingers around its spine.

The chill crept under Fosse's cuff and crawled into his skin. It gripped at his body, clawed at his bones and seeped into his very soul. His arms ached. Heavy, sinking in the icy flow, his right arm pulled under. His head swam. Each laboured breath dragged in the smell of fresh earth.

He cracked open one eye. Blackness surrounded him. A soft rustle trickled down from above. A brisk breeze snatched at his coat.

Where am I?

A rustling below him. He held out his free arm and probed into the dark. Thick leaves slapped against his fingers.

Outside.

Fosse raised his head. Faint shadows danced against the night sky. A new moon hid in the heavens.

No help there.

The breeze died.

A soft thump broke the silence. Another. A series of thuds rolled toward him. A hazy light bobbed among the silhouetted tree trunks, grew larger.

Fosse stretched out his left arm and groped the air. Metal fingers scraped. Shards of bark showered over his face. He dragged himself to the opposite side.

The pool of light swayed along the ground. The will-o-wisp floated closer.

He waited.

The lamp wormed and flickered its way through a copse of trunks.

Closer.

It froze, just a few yards away. It floated higher, illuminating a cloaked figure, then a familiar face.

Beattie!

Fosse dragged himself along the trunk. He stumbled toward the pool of light.

"What are you doing here?"

"Edgar!" Beatrice grinned and threw out her arms.

And halted mid-step.

"What's the matter, Beattie?"

Beatrice stepped back and held her lamp at arm's length.

"What have you done, Edgar?" she asked.

Fosse dragged his foot forward and tried to lift his arms against the tide of tired, aching muscles. His shoulders drooped.

"Where are we?" he asked.

"Don't play games, Edgar."

"Games?"

Beatrice's gaze flicked to one side. Her eyes widened and slowly turned back toward him.

"You don't remember anything?" she asked.

"Remember what?" His head spun. He needed to sit down.

"I remember going to my study after dinner." He closed his eyes. *Then nothing.* "Then I was here."

Beatrice frowned and lifted the lamp closer, illuminating his right arm.

"Edgar, put the shovel down please."

Fosse opened his eyes. His white knuckles gripped an iron shovel. He flicked his fingers open. The shovel clunked to the ground, next to the mound of newly dug dirt.

He swallowed.

Beatrice stepped closer to the mound.

"Don't," he whispered.

She leaned forward and gasped.

"Is there…?" asked Fosse. His stomach lurched into his throat.

Beatrice nodded.

"Who is it?"

"I don't recognise him," she replied.

Him? Fosse's stomach sank. *Then there is a body.* He took a long breath and peeked into the shallow grave. A dark suit was soiled with blood. A bandaged hand gripped the ground. A young man's face stared back at him, hair matted with blood.

"Turner?" Fosse's voice cracked.

"You know him?"

"He works…" Fosse cleared his throat and stumbled back into a tree. He leaned against the trunk. "He worked for me at the Museum."

Beatrice rocked back on her heels and stared at him.

"Edgar, my sweet. Why?"

"I didn't–" *Why can't I remember?*

Beatrice's eyes locked onto the shovel.

"Are you sure? This is not the first time your memory has failed you, my sweet."

He squeezed his eyes shut.

Not again.

He remembered dinner: turtle soup, roast beef, potatoes and asparagus. He remembered a glass of sweet port by the fire in his study. He remembered the warm, earthy aroma of his favourite pipe–.

The breeze bit his face. He regarded his wife through a veil of tears. There were so many gaps in his memory now.

Why can't I remember?

"Just like your uncle?" asked Beatrice. "And now he's…"

Metal fingers whirred and rattled. Fosse squeezed them until they silenced. Memory loss had been the first sign of his uncle's affliction.

"Edgar. You can't follow your uncle into Bedlam and leave me alone." Beatrice lowered the lamp. Long shadows flooded the grave.

Fosse's leg buckled. He fell to his knees.

I am not going mad. I will not end up in Bedlam.

He clutched the shovel and scraped a pile of dirt into the hole.

The leaves shook around them. Fragments of earth stung Fosse's face and dug themselves into his eyes.

A faint whistle twisted on the breeze.

His muscles froze. *Police?*

"We must go," whispered Beatrice.

The shrill of whistles circled closer.

"Edgar." The lamp light went out. "We must go now!"

A hand grasped his elbow and dragged him away into the night; the shovel scraped along the ground behind him.

Chapter 2:
Down the Rabbit Hole

Wheels squeaked in the hall outside the autopsy room. Viola pushed open the door. Jones entered; the metal gurney rumbled over the tiles to the centre of the room. A bulging paper bag jiggled on the linen covering.

"Good morning, Constable Jones," said Viola.

Constable Jones helped Henry slip the corpse onto the autopsy table.

"Morning, Doctor Stewart." Jones nodded, passed her the paper bag and absconded into the hall, clicking the door shut behind him.

"Why is he always in a hurry?" asked Viola

"He's terrified you will chastise him." Henry chuckled. "Again."

Viola crossed to the far bench, turned her back on Henry and smirked.

Poor man.

She emptied the paper bag and spread the victim's belongings into a tray: a cheap pocket watch, three crowns and a silver medallion in the shape of a falcon.

Viola held the trinket up and flipped it.

Curious.

Viola returned to Henry's side and presented the amulet.

"Henry, look at this." The medallion glinted in the shaft of sunlight from the roof casement. "It's a falcon amulet."

"Like the one found on the other corpse?"

"Yes, just like the one on the Man in Grey," replied Viola.

Henry slipped the linen cover off the body and glanced in Viola's direction.

"The Man in–?" His frowned as his stethoscope clattered onto the table.

"Yes, he's one of *them*!" she replied.

"Viola, just because the man had a grey suit does not make him a member of The Society. It's a popular colour."

Henry's moustache twitched. Viola knew there was a smirk hidden beneath the meticulously waxed affectation.

"I have a grey suit," he said.

He hummed as he lifted the corpse's left arm and wiggled it.

No rigor mortis yet. Viola examined the body. A long gash blemished the torso. A tattered handkerchief wrapped round one hand.

Viola gasped.

"Well, I do. It befits my burgundy waistcoat."

"No, Henry!" She waved her finger in the direction of the body. "Look."

Clods of earth clung to the hair. A layer of grime covered the face.

Henry flipped through the Constabulary notes.

"The poor fellow was found half-buried in a grave," he said.

"But don't you recognise him, Henry? It's the young man from the Lecture Hall."

Henry grabbed a sponge and wiped some dirt from the cheeks. He peered at the face and pursed his lips. "Are you certain?"

"Yes." Viola grabbed the bandaged hand and turned it over. She tugged at the dressing. A crust of dry blood fell away from a gash on the palm.

"He was Mr Chartha's assistant at the mummy unwrapping. He injured his hand removing the lid. Remember?"

Henry parted the matted hair, plucked out a lump of earth and plopped it in the metal bowl at the foot of the table.

First the Man in Grey, now Turner. Perhaps there is a curse.

Viola surveyed the dirt.

"Where was he found?" she asked.

Henry skimmed the notes. "In a shallow grave in the old St George's cemetery."

The blood chilled in her arteries and shot down her arm. She could almost hear the moaning of the apparition from her sitting room, see Anne pulled into the ground.

He was buried in the ground. Like Anne. Viola swallowed, trying to quell the rising nausea.

Impossible! It has to be a coincidence. Her arm muscles spasmed.

Perhaps I am going mad? Perhaps that is my curse?

Viola wiped dirt off her leather apron.

"I think his name was Turner," she said.

Henry resumed a faltering tune, humming as he rolled the sod between his fingers. He frowned. The tune died. He slipped his finger under the tresses and lifted a lock of hair.

"Hand me the chisel."

Henry scrutinised the skull. He slipped the chisel into the bone and prised off the skullcap.

"Another one?" whispered Viola, as she held out the bowl.

Henry nodded.

"One is unique, perhaps a curiosity. Two is coincidence, though I think very unlikely."

Coincidence. Yes, it has to be. She shivered. *Three times is the curse.*

The skullcap clattered into the bowl. Henry flicked traces of congealed mud and blood from the flesh inside the cranium. A crack opened along the grey matter. The two lobes separated, with a squelch.

"I wonder…?" said Henry.

He prodded at the exposed edge and mumbled: "That's interesting."

Viola leaned closer. The pineal gland was noticeable by its absence.

Tendrils wrapped around Viola's chest. They tightened. Her heart thumped, trying to beat free of its constrictive cage.

Not a coincidence.

She studied the mid-brain. The shape of the surrounding tissue looked familiar.

It almost looks like…

The folds of the tissue formed the rough shape of an eye. Pages flicked in her mind as she sifted through the memory of the paintings and hieroglyphs recorded in the Professor's textbook.

"Henry, if I use my imagination," she leaned closer, "that almost looks like the Eye of Horus," she said.

"The what?" replied Henry.

"The Egyptian eye Professor Fosse showed us." She traced her finger along the edges. "See?"

Henry wiped the crumbling soil off his hands and tossed the linen cloth into a nearby hamper.

"I blame Doyle," he sighed. "That's what comes from reading those fantastical boo–" Henry paused. He squinted at the corpse and bit his lip. "Unfortunately your imagination has a way of rubbing off on others," he continued.

They hovered over the corpse. Henry grasped the scalpel.

The corpse shuddered.

Viola jumped. The medallion slipped from her fingers and clinked on the tiled floor. Her cheeks burned.

Calm down. You've seen corpses spasm before. It's to be expected.

She bent down and scooped up the medallion. Light flashed across her vision. Viola braced herself for another apparition. The image of the Man in Grey and the sarcophagus lid skipped through her memory. The painted Eye stared back her, its centre red and raging.

"Henry." She curled her fingers around the medallion and squeezed. "There was an eye on the sarcophagus lid, at the unwrapping."

"Then, we need to take a closer look at that sarcophagus," replied

Henry.

The brick staircase led down to the Marylebone Station cellar. Viola's skirts brushed along the wall. She ducked under the lintel of the doorway and followed Henry. Constable Jones led them into the darkness, a crowbar dangling from his fist.

Jones scrabbled along one wall. A loud click. A hiss and the chamber erupted with a blue-tinged light.

Steam drizzled from the seams of a small cast iron *Moisture-Depleting Combustor Generator* stuffed into an alcove near the bottom step. The humidity dropped as they reached the cellar floor. Viola swallowed. The air seemed to suck the moisture from her every pore.

Pipes chugged above their heads, hugging the low ceiling.

Another effort to ward off the destructive damp?

Jones slipped off his helmet to avoid the pipes. Henry stooped to follow him.

They entered a pool of light cast by a vertical lighting cylinder. Fine blue sparks crackled inside the glass casing, dancing along a filament. Thin copper pipes emerged from the contraption and buried themselves in the brickwork wall.

"I've heard of these," said Viola. "It works with electrical current, doesn't it?"

Jones shrugged and wandered off down an aisle between the stacked crates.

"Henry, why don't you get some electricity for the morgue? We wouldn't be restricted to daylight hours."

Henry skirted around the tube. "I'm not sure it's safe, Viola. Besides, the permits are too expensive."

Viola frowned. "Then why does the cellar have it?"

"Removing the damp protects the evidence stored down here," replied Henry. "Gas lighting also increases the risk of fire. A recent series of less than fortuitous events caused the loss of key pieces of evidence." He lowered his voice to a whisper. "Some of which had great import to The Crown. It was deemed necessary to have alternative lighting." He raised an eyebrow. "The Queen signed the papers herself."

Viola glanced over the seemingly haphazard array of crates. Cloth-covered intrigues stood amongst tables filled with glass-entombed objects.

"Surely if something was that important, it would be in the possession of The Crown?" she asked.

"Apparently not." replied Henry. He cocked his head at a most uncomfortable-looking angle to avoid a low-lying pipe.

"But–"

"Over here, Doctor Collins." The makeshift walls muffled Jones' voice.

Viola slipped past Henry and hurried down the aisle. Henry shoved his hands in his trouser pockets and followed.

Jones stood a respectable distance from the sarcophagus, in a cloud of steam. A wheeled box-engine beside him belched out more vapour. A portable lighting tube hummed at the foot of the sarcophagus.

Viola glanced at the sarcophagus, then to the cowering Constable. Jones stared past her toward the funerary box and rubbed his chin.

"I'll not be risking a curse," he whispered. He edged a few steps closer to the stairs.

"Come on, man," said Henry. "You can't possibly believe it's cursed?"

"Sir, you have two bodies in the morgue already. I don't wish to join them." He cleared his throat and swallowed. "Still, unless you order me to stay, sir…"

He handed a crowbar to Henry and retreated another step.

"I thought the curse affected only those who opened a sarcophagus?" asked Viola.

"And anyone present." Jones' voice was shaky. "Or, so I'm told."

Viola's pulse quickened.

"Tosh," snorted Henry.

"I don't need to open it," said Viola. "I just need to examine the lid." She took a deep breath and stepped up to the sarcophagus. The paint no longer glistened. Viola stretched out her fingers to check.

And paused. Last time she had touched it, she had seen the strange shadowy apparition.

The paint is dry now. Surely, it's safe?

The eye's scarlet iris seemed to stare back at her. Her throat burned. She licked her dry lips.

She curled her fingers away from the lid and withdrew her hand.

"See the resemblance, Henry?"

Henry examined the pictograph.

"Hmmm. Yes, I suppose the folds of the midbrain do resemble the symbol," he replied.

"The heart of the soul. That is what Professor Fosse calls it. Mrs Fosse said her husband is fanatical about it."

Henry raised an eyebrow. "Fanatical?"

"Those were her exact words. Apparently, he's fixated on what happens when we are dead. He's even consulted a spiritualist."

"Hmmm."

Viola peered at the pictograph. The eye was deliberately painted over the cartouche.

"Henry, I think the eye was added later."

Henry leaned closer and examined the markings.

"You're correct. But when, and why? And by whom?"

"Don't they photograph artefacts to record their discovery?" she replied.

Henry nodded.

"Jones, did Professor Fosse provide any reference photographs for the investigation?" he asked.

Jones circled around the coffin, almost clinging to the wall of boxes surrounding them. He slipped down another makeshift aisle. He returned, pausing at the last pile of boxes, and thrust a large file bound with string in Henry's direction.

Henry rolled his eyes and snatched the file from Jones' grasp, slipped the string off it and sifted through the contents. Viola examined the contents past his shoulder.

Of particular note were several photographs, one of the Professor and an older man holding digging tools. Another showed a tomb, the walls covered in paintings of a jackal-headed human holding a scale, with the intact sarcophagus in situ. There were several of the coffin itself; one of it in its entirety. The others were magnified, detailing the hieroglyphs covering its sides and lid.

Viola tapped the photograph with her finger.

"There's no eye on the lid," she said.

"It must've been added sometime after the photograph was taken. But when?" asked Henry.

Viola rubbed her thumb over her fingers. The paint had been wet at the unwrapping. She sniffed the paint.

Linseed.

"It smells like artist oils," she said. "They can take a couple of days or weeks to touch dry. But the body was possibly only a few days old."

Henry wiped his finger over the pictograph.

"It's dry. It may not be related to our body but we still need to record the graffito as evidence."

Viola struggled to slow her breath.

I'm certain the pigment was wet.

"Jones, organise the photographic equipment. You can help Doctor

Stewart."

Jones nodded and dashed through the maze of boxes toward the stairs.

"The man is a bundle of nerves," said Henry.

"He's scared," replied Viola. A slow breath escaped her lips. "What if there really is a curse?"

Henry shook his head and sighed.

"Jones has a vivid imagination, Viola."

Viola grabbed Henry's arm. Her heart thumped in her chest.

"But, Henry." She tried not to squeeze. "The boy, Turner, helped open the coffin. Now he's dead. He was buried. Just like..."

She could never forget the vision of Anne, her hand clawing at a grave mound, dirt on her face.

"I was there, Henry. Right next to the coffin. I moved the lid."

Henry's moustache drooped. Creases formed in the corners of his eyes and between his brows. He turned to face Viola, placed her hands in his, and spoke in a slow, clear voice:

"You didn't open it, Vi."

"But I did. I–" She struggled to confine her hammering heart in its ribbed cage.

"No." He squeezed her hands gently. "The original mummy was replaced. Remember?"

Viola stared at him. She blinked slowly. Her mind was numb. She could think of nothing but moaning shadows, stumbling mummies and her sister - Anne - sinking into a carpet of earth.

"Someone had already opened the coffin, removed the mummy and replaced it with your Man in Grey."

Henry's piercing blue eyes stared into hers, not moving.

"If anyone is cursed, it is the one who first opened the sarcophagus, Viola. Most likely our murderer. We shall find him and he will hang. He has cursed himself.

I think I need to talk with Professor Fosse tomorrow," he said.

Viola's mind raced. It spun under a heavy weight. Her forehead fell onto Henry's shoulder.

Who was the murderer? Who opened the sarcophagus? Who had access to it? Professor Fosse? But what was his motive? What did the Eye of Horus have to do with it? Where was the mummy? Where was–? Anne!

Henry's hand caressed her hair. Slow. Soothing. She listened to his beating heart.

Thump.

Thump.

Her heart slowed to beat in time with his.

Thump.

Sunlight streamed across the ecru carpet runner in the hall. Shadows formed dunes, valleys and ripples in its deep pile. Fosse's feet sank into the wool, as if in loose sand. He missed the squelch of the desert sand, missed the hot wind on his face, and missed the exhilaration of uncovering the secrets of an untouched tomb.

Carved sandstone heads rested on columns, on either side of the hallstand; mementos of his first excavations in Tanis. He snatched his battered wide-brimmed hat from the stand, plopped it on his head and pulled the telescoped-crown snug. He closed his eyes and took a deep breath. The straw smelled of dust and crumbling sandstone. He smiled. If only Beattie would return to Egypt with him...

The crown tugged his hair as the hat was whisked from his head. Fosse's eyes snapped open. Beatrice glared at him, her face almost as bright as the pleated concoction of scarlet velvet, tassels and braid that swathed her full figure.

"You're not wearing that old thing to your meeting," she said. "And that suit–" Her gaze tracked down to his pale linen suit. "You're not in Egypt anymore, Edgar. London society has standards. Perhaps a nice grey suit? They're quite fashionable at the moment."

Beatrice hung his hat on the stand and offered him another.

Fosse stared at the grey bowler hat.

"You've gone pale, Edgar. What's the matter?" she asked.

"That's not mine, Beattie. It belongs to–" He swallowed.

"Oh, the–" Beatrice bit her lip and shoved the bowler into her carpetbag hidden in a hallstand box. "There, it's gone. We won't speak of it again."

Fosse's stomach lurched. A metallic click jittered under his sleeve. He clenched his mechanical hand. Gears whirred in protest.

"Beattie…" he whispered. "I don't want to hang."

"You won't, my love."

Beatrice pulled out a pair of leather gloves from her pocket, and slipped them onto his hands. She clasped his metallic hand.

"Haven't I always looked after you?" Beatrice smiled.

Fosse nodded. "I don't know what I'd do without you, Beattie. You've been my rock, since Edward died." He wrapped his flesh hand around Beatrice's, trying to shake the memory of his dying son.

Beatrice's smile slipped. Her hands fell to her side.

"I'm so sorry, dearest. I shouldn't have mentioned…" Fosse's mechanical hand chittered.

Beatrice winced. She took a deep breath, pulled at the hem of her bodice and frowned.

"If only you hadn't placed the body in the sarcophagus. That wasn't smart, Edgar. Who else would have access to the mummy?"

Fosse's breaths quickened.

"But… But, what if they come back?" He grabbed Beatrice's hand. "What if they question me again?" He struggled to breathe. "What if they find out I wasn't in Scotland during the unwrapping?"

"Just keep to our story," replied Beatrice.

"But they know he was here, Beattie!" Fosse's hand trembled.

"Hush, my dear. They don't suspect a thing." Beatrice extracted her hand and straightened his cravat. "Trust me."

"And I can't remember doing these terrible things." Fosse shook his head. "Why did I do them?"

"You must have had your reasons," replied Beatrice. "Perhaps Mr Turner was stealing your research? I never did trust him."

"And Mr Umber?"

The smile returned to Beatrice's lips.

"That was his fault - trying to trick you out of your inheritance. It's fortunate his real intentions were discovered, or we'd be in the poor house now."

Fosse's hand clicked and whirred, settling into a fast-paced rhythm.

"What if they find his bowler?" he gasped.

"Hush, now. They won't." Her voice slithered like treacle.

"What else will they find?" asked Fosse. "What have I forgotten?"

"Don't worry, they didn't suspect Lord Banbury, for years," whispered Beatrice.

Uncle Eustace? The echoing screams of Bedlam still haunted his memory. *Why would she mention him?* He eyed his beloved wife; she avoided his direct gaze.

Is she scared of me? His lungs refused to breathe. *What if I can't control myself!*

"Oh, God, what if I hurt you, Beattie?" The words caught in his throat.

"You wouldn't hurt me," she replied as she straightened his coat.

"But, what if I—"

"Hush. It will be all right." She placed a hand on each side of his face. "I trust you, Edgar. I know you better than you do yourself."

"What did I do to deserve you, dearest?" The whirring slowed. Beatrice kissed him on the cheek. Fosse's breathing slowed. "Any loving wife would support her husband, my dear."

A large sarcophagus stood guard near the entrance of the study. Two lacquered eyes surveyed the room, their lapis irises flat. They seemed to follow Viola as she crossed Professor Fosse's study. Flat. Cold. Accusing. Viola shivered and tightened her hold on Henry's elbow.

An extensive collection of Egyptian artefacts and curios filled the locked bookshelves. More were stuffed into glass-fronted curiosity cabinets. Knick-knacks covered almost every available surface - all except the mantelpiece: only two Egyptian statuettes flanked a silver-framed tintype.

Viola took a deep breath; the hot air dried her nostrils. She glanced at the crackling fire. It was late in the year for a fire during the day.

Perhaps the Professor's time in Egypt has sensitised him to the cold?

Fosse stood by the full-length bay window, surrounded by a jungle of luscious palm leaves, and stared into the street. The leaves waved in the breeze, tapping his shoulders in rhythm with each flurry through the open crevice of the central sash.

He'd look like a big-game hunter searching out his prey, if he weren't so bookish. Viola bit her lip. She was a guest in the Professor's house. *She*, at least, would observe social courtesy.

Fosse's gloved hand whirred as he flexed his fingers.

"May I congratulate you on your extensive collection, Professor Fosse?" said Henry.

"Thank you, Doctor Collins." Fosse clenched his gloved fist and turned to face Henry. A hint of silver glinted at his throat as he adjusted his dishevelled cravat. "I miss Egypt. This is my comfort, my very own piece of The Nile."

His ungloved fingers lingered on his cravat as his gaze flickered over Viola, pausing for a moment on her eyepatch, before settling back on Henry. His mechanical hand twitched by his side. He snatched his ungloved hand away from his neck, and shoved his mechanical hand into his jacket pocket as he stepped behind his desk.

"Of course the cream of the artefacts are to be part of the Museum display." He adjusted a model obelisk on his desk. "Did you receive your invitation to the opening, Doctor Stewart?"

"Ah, yes. Thank you," replied Viola.

"I must apologise for the unforeseen events at the unwrapping. I do hope the exhibit will make up for any disappointment." Fosse swallowed and smiled. "Please, sit."

He indicated an eclectic array of chairs surrounding his desk. A tapestried *chaise transatlantique*, a leather-seated Egyptian stool with a tassel at each corner and an uncomfortable looking high-backed, wooden chair carved with stylised lotus leaves and storks.

Henry stretched out his arm, offering Viola the more traditional seat. Viola sank into the tapestry-covered chair, struggling to keep her balance as she shuffled to get comfortable.

Definitely not made for bustle skirts.

The sarcophagus stared blankly at Viola, as if listening to every word. Judging her.

Viola swivelled toward the windows to avoid its gaze. Three tall terrariums stood where Fosse had been, flanked either side by palms. White, purple and blue flowers glowed in the morning sun. Black berries glinted among muted leaves.

"Beautiful specimens, Professor Fosse. I assume the warmth aids in their growth?" asked Viola. "I must admit I have a black thumb."

"As do I, Doctor Stewart." Fosse ran his hand along a strappy palm leaf next to him. "I am lost when it comes to Botany. These are my wife's specimens."

"Yes, Mrs Fosse was kind enough to suggest some books on the subject."

Henry settled on the Egyptian stool and placed his doctor's bag on the floor beside him.

Fosse lowered himself into his desk chair and turned to Henry.

"Doctor Collins, I do hope the sarcophagus will be released in time for the opening. The public, and indeed Her Majesty, will be expecting it."

Henry cleared his throat.

"I can't give you my guarantee, Professor. It is evidence in a murder enquiry."

"But surely an exception can be made? It is the centre of the new exhibit." His hand chittered in his pocket.

"I'm afraid it's not my decision."

"Ah." Fosse frowned and re-organised a pile of papers on the desk. A photograph of a treasure-filled tomb slipped from the pile.

The sarcophagus!

"The sarcophagus is the precise reason for our visit, Professor Fosse," Viola glanced in Henry's direction.

"How can I be of help?" asked Fosse.

Henry pulled a photograph from his coat pocket and slipped it onto the desk.

"We have found an irregularity on the sarcophagus and are in need of your expertise," replied Henry.

"There are some markings that don't appear to be part of the original design," added Viola.

Fosse removed the mechanical hand from his pocket and slid open a desk drawer to retrieve a small magnifying loupe. He wedged it in front of his eye, twisted it into the eye socket and picked up the photograph. His eyes widened, the loupe wobbled for an instant as the eyebrow's grip loosened, then fell into Fosse's ungloved hand. The corners of his mouth drooped slightly. Fosse licked his lips and leaned slowly back into his chair, still staring at the image.

Viola narrowed her eye and regarded Fosse.

"Is something wrong, Professor?" she asked.

Fosse's gloved hand whirred and twitched toward his throat and froze. He lowered it slowly, palm down on the table. The tremor abated. He glared at Henry.

"It's an outrage! Someone has defaced a priceless artefact. I demand your Constabulary find the culprit at once."

Viola raised an eyebrow. *He has a temper. But I need the information.*

"Professor, the symbol?" said Viola.

"Yes," replied Henry, "what is the significance of The Eye of Horus?"

Fosse's eyes widened.

"Horus?" He shook his head and swallowed. "No, *this* is the Eye of Ra."

That can't be.

"But I thought...?" Viola squirmed forward on her chair.

Fosse avoided Viola's gaze.

"A common mistake." He pressed his index finger onto the photograph and pushed it toward them. "If you look closely, you'll see this is a left eye. The Eye of Horus is depicted as a right eye. *This* is the Eye of Ra."

"Is there a difference?" asked Henry.

Fosse glared at Henry as he withdrew his hand, took a long breath and placed both hands on the table, steady and unmoving.

"Horus is the god of healing, rumoured to restore life to the dead - *'head of a falcon, skin of a man'*. His Eye is common enough in burials."

Viola gasped. *Head of a falcon. Skin of a man. Could that have been the shadowy figure in the Lecture Hall?*

Henry placed a gentle hand on hers; the warmth embraced her fingers.

He cocked his head in her direction. A reassuring smile flickered across his lips. Viola looked into his eyes. They remained calm, though faint lines crept across his forehead. She wasn't fooled. He was still worried.

"And the Eye of Ra?" she asked, hoping her voice would not betray her trepidation.

Fosse rose slowly from his chair and turned to the window.

"It is associated with the lion-headed goddess, Bast," he replied. "Also known as the Lady of the Flame, or the Devouring Lady."

"That doesn't bode well," said Henry.

"She is the agent of action." Fosse paused and folded his arms. "The Bringer of Wrath. She protects her own."

"*Wrath*?" echoed Viola. "As in curse?"

"Curse?" Fosse spun on his heel to face them. His eyes narrowed and flicked from Viola to Henry. "He whosoever shall disturb my rest?" He chuckled. "Hmmm."

The palms shivered. Shadows flickered across the floor. Viola's heart thumped.

"There are many incidents documented." Fosse fingered the cravat at his neck and stared past them in the direction of the guard-sarcophagus. His mechanical hand rattled. "But I have protection. The children of Ra will not have me."

Viola struggled to breathe. She shifted in her chair. Pain shot along her chest and down her arm. Her hand trembled. Henry gently squeezed Viola's hand.

"You talk as if you believe this balderdash. Surely, as a man of science, you don't truly believe in the curse legends?" asked Henry.

Fosse eyed Viola out of the corner of his eye. He blinked slowly and returned his attention to Henry.

"I must apologise," he replied calmly. "The ladies usually enjoy the titillation. Or so I'm told; Mrs Fosse says most expect a good ghost story when they attend the lecture tour at the Museum." He bowed in

Viola's direction. "She says I do go too far sometimes. Please accept my apologies, Doctor Stewart."

Why don't I believe you?

Henry raised an eyebrow.

The study door clicked. China rattled as the maid deposited the tea tray on a side table. Beatrice followed her and sat in the remaining chair.

"Tea anyone?" asked Fosse with a crooked smile.

The dressing table drawer scraped. Viola winced. She reached her fingers inside and dragged out its contents. She placed the cache of letters bound with a red silk ribbon on the dressing table. Each letter bore her name, each neatly opened, its contents read and carefully returned to the original envelope preserved for posterity.

Viola unwrapped the bundle and trailed her hand over the top letter. It was signed in a confident hand.

Henry Collins.

She had been so spellbound by their courtship she had neglected something very important.

Viola brushed her loose auburn curls behind her shoulder. She adjusted her eye patch and took a deep breath.

She palmed a thinner collection of letters from the bottom of the bundle. The handwriting was finer, more delicate. She untied the black ribbon, unfolded the paper and read the faint signature.

Anne Carrington.

Viola stared at the letter. Air rushed from her lungs as if she had been kicked in the chest. She caught her breath.

How could I have forgotten?

It had been months since she had read Anne's letter. Now she could not tear her eyes from it.

I have abandoned you.

Her eyes stung. Tears crept along her lower eyelid.

I have abandoned you for Henry. For my own happiness.

A tear tumbled onto the paper, spreading like veins along its compacted fibres.

The gas lamp flickered on the wall behind her. Shadows flitted over the dressing table. A faint smell of flowers lingered. The muslin curtain fluttered in the breeze.

<Why did you forsake me?> Anne's voice whispered on the breeze.

Please, forgive me, Anne.

<You buried my memory.> A soft breeze tickled her ear.

Viola dragged her attention toward the mirror. Shadows mixed with tears, obscuring her reflection. Viola blinked. Tears spilled onto her cheeks. She stared at her image.

Anne's pale face stared back.

<Why did you forsake me?>

A cold shiver knifed down her spine. It bored into her chest and choked her heart. Viola opened her mouth to cry out.

Silence.

Her breath escaped.

Letters scattered over the table. Viola clutched at Anne's letter. It fluttered to the floor.

Light flashed across the mirror. Viola's attention snapped back to the glass.

Viola blinked. She held her breath as she scanned the reflection.

She was alone.

Her heart skipped, tentatively picking up its beat. She wiped her cheek. Her eyelids fluttered. It had been a long day.

Henry was right. I need rest.

She leaned down and brushed a speck of dirt off Anne's letter.

And there's no such thing as curses.

Viola's fingers curled around the paper. Grains of dirt trickled to the floor.

A shimmer of iridescent silk brushed against her face.

The air was still.

Viola peeked out the corner of her eye. Fine silk gauze floated around her. Her gaze crept up the shroud of silk to its cowl-like peak.

Viola swallowed.

The cowl twisted toward her and peeled away. Pale amber eyes stared back at her.

Viola sat bolt upright. A chill slammed around her.

"Anne?" Viola's voice cracked.

<Why did you give up, Viola?> Anne blinked. Her mouth remained unmoving.

"I... I..." Viola's chest tightened.

<You had two admirers. I had no-one. You could've spared one for me.>

Viola's hands gripped the edge of the dressing table. Each breath laboured against an unseen weight.

<You won your husband and forgot about me.>

"Anne, I ..." The room blurred in a flurry of tears.

<Now you have another sweetheart and have forgotten me again.>

Viola struggled to liberate her breath.

I'm sorry, Anne.

Anne held out a bloodless arm towards Viola's chest.

<Why didn't you save me?>

Viola wheezed. Her head spun. How could she have married Donell and forgotten her sister? How could she now marry Henry and forget her again? A sliver of ice pierced her heart. She opened her mouth. A pale wisp of breath escaped. Silence. Viola licked the salt from her lips.

How could I?

The grip on her chest loosened slightly. Anne turned and drifted behind Viola's chair.

Viola sipped the air and peeked into the mirror.

Anne's eyes narrowed. <You owe me a debt.>

Viola nodded slowly.

Anne's eyes widened - the right blurred in shadow, the left black and shiny. A translucent membrane flicked horizontally across the surface of the remaining eye. Anne's face dissolved, melding into Viola's reflection, its thin wispy edges caught in an eddy and twisted in the air.

A sharp-curved beak erupted through the apparition. Feathers and bone shook off the mist. The membrane flicked across the shiny cornea again. The eye stared at Viola, its partner missing - gouged out from the skull.

The wind curled around Viola, lifting her hair and twirling it around her throat.

"No!" The scream lingered, snatched away as the wind sped toward the open window.

Viola's chair toppled and shot across the floor. She fell and scuttled away from the table, toward the bed. She grabbed at the bed covers behind her back, scrambled along the edge of the bed and pulled herself to her feet.

The curtains flinched in the wind, fanning the wall lamps. Shadows shifted over the room... And over the falcon-headed creature that loomed over her. A large golden disc crowned its head. Linen cloths swaddled the muscular body of a half-naked man.

"Head of a falcon, skin of a man." Viola's forehead tightened. *Horus?*

Horus lifted his arm and pointed at her eye socket, entombed behind the silk eyepatch.

No.

Viola's calves knocked against the wooden boards of the bed. She grabbed a bed post and swivelled her body onto the bed, trying to use the post as a shield.

The stench of stale Frankincense clawed at her throat. She swallowed. A bitter taste remained.

Edges of Horus's linen skirt lifted, straps unravelled, floated in the air and snaked toward Viola.

"You're not real!" She clutched at the bed clothes. *You can't exist.*

Horus glided closer. Long talons scratched at the air. His index finger glistened gold in the lamplight. He paused. An empty socket regarded Viola. He cocked his head. The disc on his head blazed.

Magnified light stabbed at Viola's eye. She winced, unable to escape.

Horus continued toward her. Fluid. Gliding.

Closer.

Viola groped blindly under the bed linens, searching for the bed warmer.

Nothing.

She flailed at the side table, searching for any sort of weapon. Her fingernails scraped, ripping on the wood.

Nothing.

Viola held her breath.

There's no such thing as a curse.

Linen tendrils tapped at her shoulders and wrapped around her waist. They clasped tight, squeezing the air from her lungs, dragging her closer to the falcon-headed form. Metal talons scraped at the silk of her eye patch, caught on the lace edging, shredded the threads and sank into her empty socket.

Viola gasped for air.

Henry, I trusted you!

Warm air breathed over her face. She closed her eye and squeezed her eyelid tight.

"No!" The scream echoed around her.

The breath warmed, skimming over Viola's neck. She struggled to turn her head away. A soft growl echoed in her ear.

Heat pressed against her body, tearing into her skin.

Viola's eye snapped wide open.

The air sucked from Viola's lungs. It sped toward the open window, taking with it the warming light.

The walls banged. The door pounded, muffled voices barely audible outside.

Viola closed her eye. A whiff of gas tickled her nose.

A buzzing filled Viola's head. Thoughts swirled and faded. Words rose above the swarm, bobbing on the edge of her consciousness.

Mad...

Curse...

Bedlam...

Viola's head thumped. Blood rushed through her ears. She tried to focus on the words, to catch them. They slipped away, melting back into the jumbled swarm.

Her eyelid twitched, refusing to open.

More words bubbled in her subconscious, refusing to surface.

"She's rambling, sir," It was Polly. "Something about mummies, monsters and…" Her voice fell to a whisper, barely audible. "And naked men."

Viola could almost hear her blush.

"Oh sir, if anyone hears… They'll ship her off to the madhouse."

No!

"Don't worry, Polly. She's not going to Bedlam." Henry's voice was calm, soothing. "I won't–"

Viola gasped for a breath. Pains crawled through her chest.

"Viola?" Henry's hand fell softly onto her shoulder.

Viola prised her eyelid open. Morning light trickled through the open window, bathing Viola in a patch of sunlight. Light seared through her cornea, squirming down the optic nerve.

Henry's face loomed above her, hazy. She tried to focus. Her eye ached. Her eyelid snapped shut.

"Viola, can you hear me?" Henry's moustache dropped. His hand wrapped gently around Viola's forehead.

Henry shook his head, turned and whispered to Polly.

"She has a fever."

Polly's white cap bobbed.

The corners of Henry's mouth twitched. Blurred smile lines in his forehead formed but no reassuring crinkles licked the corner of his eyes.

Viola mumbled. Her words choked in her throat. *He's worried.*

Viola struggled to sit up. The room flipped and spun. She plopped back on the bed and struggled to focus. The night table rolled into view. On it sat Fosse's Egyptology book with her eyepatch placed on top, cords neatly folded underneath it.

Viola glared at the book. *How did it get there?* She'd left it in the library.

Henry glanced at the night table, frowned and turned back to Polly.

"That could explain the subject of her delirium," he said. "I'll return it to Professor Fosse tomorrow."

A chilled breeze swept over Viola's skin. Her lungs spasmed.

"Sir, she will catch a chill," pleaded Polly.

"We need it open to flush out any lingering gas," he replied.

Polly moved out of view. A door scraped.

A warm weight cloaked Viola's body. Nimble fingers tucked under her, pulling the weight tighter, constricting her movement, pressing on her lungs. Viola's pulse quickened. Her muscles twitched. Her throat clenched, quashing her scream.

Henry's smiling face leaned closer, still foggy around the edges. The comforting scent of vanilla and new leather filled her lungs, embraced her. Calmed her. She drank it in.

Henry. The urge to scream faded.

Viola's vision began to clear. Polly hovered behind Henry, wringing the edge of her apron.

"Don't fuss, Polly," he said. "She just needs clean air and rest."

Polly straightened her cap, brushed down her apron and sighed.

"I'll fetch some tea."

Henry raised an eyebrow. "And some cake."

"Of course, sir." Polly smiled and opened the bedroom door.

Henry loosened the blanket and took Viola's hand.

"You're safe now. You're lucky Polly returned early."

"If it weren't for that storm…" said Polly. She shook her head and clicked the door shut behind her.

Henry ran his hand over Viola's hair.

Calm.

Viola's breathing slowed.

Movement flickered in the corner of her eye. Shadows moved closer. Her gaze flicked to the night table.

She didn't have a fever. It wasn't delirium.

She was cursed. Or going mad. Either way, there was but one fate. Henry couldn't save her, for all his doctoring.

"Am I…" asked Viola in a raspy voice." Am I mad, Henry?"

"Never, Viola," he replied.

"Promise?"

"There is no need. Fever delirium is well documented."

Viola swallowed. Her throat was dry.

"Henry, what if I am cursed?" she said.

Henry shook his head and patted her hand. "You are not cursed, Viola."

Viola smiled. But this wasn't the first vision she had experienced. She trusted Henry, but how could she tell him the truth?

Henry grabbed his doctor's bag.

"You need rest," he said.

The curtains fluttered and slapped against the windowsill.

Viola flinched and dug her nails into Henry's arm.

"Don't leave me," she whispered.

Henry winced. He raised an eyebrow. He lifted her fingers off his arm and interlaced his fingers with hers.

"Viola, tell me what happened?" He patted her fingers, avoiding her direct gaze. "Polly says you were attacked."

Viola gripped his fingers tighter. She nodded slowly.

"But no one was here, Viola." Henry sat on the edge of the bed. "What did you see?"

Viola's gaze darted to the night table, over the room to the window and back to Henry.

"There was–"

"There was no one here, Viola. It was just a bad dream. The wind blew out the lamps. Polly got here just in time to shut off the gas."

"But he was here. It wasn't a dream. The letters were–"

Viola glanced back to the dressing table. The letters were neatly stacked and tied with a red ribbon.

"Anne was–"

"Your sister?" Henry's palm clasped her forehead again. He bit his lip and frowned. "I'll fetch the laudanum."

No, I need a clear head.

"Please don't leave, Henry," she whispered.

"Of course not. I must look after my most treasured patient." He smiled. "And Polly is bringing cake." He chuckled, the lines still absent from around his eyes. "Everything will be better in the morning, you'll see. I'll be in after luncheon."

After visiting the Professor?

"Henry," she said. "Promise me you won't visit Professor Fosse without me,"

"I'm not sure that's a good idea. You need your rest."

"Please, Henry. Promise?"

Henry's shoulders relaxed. His eyelids were heavy, his pupils large.

"I can never refuse you, Viola."

Henry wrapped his arm around Viola's shoulders and cradled her against his chest.

"I love you, Viola."

Viola smiled and closed her eye. She breathed slowly, fighting the pain in her lungs, and tried to relax her muscles.

I just hope that's enough.

The horses twitched and kicked up the smell of fresh manure as they fidgeted at the front of the coach. Fosse paused at the coach door and tugged down the waist hem of his jacket. He preferred a lounge jacket or frock coat, if the occasion arose for it. These new dresscoats were too short. *They exposed a man. Only fit to show off.*

Beatrice skipped down their front steps. Fosse regarded her as she paraded across the footpath toward him - a vision in deep burgundy silk, trimmed with fire-red, her décolletage framed with sparkling beads and lace. He took a deep breath and smiled as he appreciated his wife's assets.

The coachman opened the coach door. Fosse offered his hand to Beatrice. She fluttered past him and bundled herself into the jiggling coach.

Fosse stooped his head and followed her inside. Her skirts spilled over the entire seat. Fosse turned, deposited himself on the padded seat opposite and pulled at his collar, trying to adjust his bow tie. Beatrice beamed at him. He returned a smile, forgetting his worries and ignoring his discomfort. He was happy.

A whip cracked overhead. The coach shuddered. Hooves clopped on the cobblestones.

"Oh, Fisher said this arrived for you." Beatrice handed him a sealed letter.

Fosse eyed the red seal. *Official looking.* His eyelids narrowed as he slipped on his spectacles, cracked the wax seal and scanned the dispatch. He sucked in a short breath; his eyelids relaxed and slowly widened. The paper quivered.

"May I?" asked Beatrice. She plucked the paper from his hands, scanned the missive and raised both eyebrows.

"Doctor Collins and Doctor Stewart want an appointment with you tomorrow afternoon?" she asked.

Fosse closed his eyes. *Why won't they leave me alone?*

The steel-rimmed wheels growled as the coach slowed, then jerked forward again, turning down a narrow lane. Fosse glanced out the window.

"Do we have to go to the party, Beattie?" he asked.

Beatrice nodded.

"It pays to be seen in the right company, my dear. Just smile and try not to mention the…" She flicked lint off his satin lapel. "…unfortunate deaths."

His mechanical hand twitched. Fosse slowly stretched out each finger in turn. Cables whirred and joints clicked as he curled them back, one by one. The clicking rhythm quickened and faltered. The hand shuddered.

Beatrice glanced at his hand, licked her lips and gazed out the window. The coach turned again. Light bathed her face. She slid open the window and turned her face into the breeze. Wisps of hair caressed her cheeks and caught the red ribbons woven into her severe bun.

"Calm down, Edgar," said Beatrice. "You know you get dyspepsia when you are upset. It's just a small party. I doubt they are acquainted with Lord Porchester."

"But *she* knows." Fosse gripped the letter, snapping the seal in his mechanical hand. "She knows!"

"Who would 'she' be, dearest?" asked Beatrice.

"That Stewart woman." He grabbed the letter and thrust it at Beatrice.

"She knows it was me." He crushed the paper in his hand. *But how? I don't even remember.*

"Viola?"

Fosse nodded slowly.

"Then I shall talk to her in the morning. She trusts me. Perhaps I can convince her you are not to blame." She straightened her skirts. "I mean, it's not your fault your family has a weakness, is it?"

Fosse pushed his spectacles back onto the bridge of his nose. *Weakness?*

"If you could only remember doing– the incidents. I would know what to say, how to defend you." She clasped his chin in her hand and sighed heavily. "Try to remember, Edgar."

"I can't, Beattie. I've tried." Metallic fingers dug into his thigh.

"How can I protect you if you can't remember?" Beatrice's shoulders slumped. "Oh Edgar, it's just like your–"

"My what?" Fosse held his breath, not wanting to hear the answer.

Beatrice's hand fell into her lap. She glanced out the window.

"Your uncle," she said.

The coach jolted, jostling Fosse, sending Beatrice's bag sliding across the polished leather seat. She snatched it up and leaned close and whispered: "The family curse."

Of course. I was with Uncle Eustace when I opened my first sarcophagus. He grabbed the edge of the window and swallowed. *When I first met Horus.*

"But surely that's forgotten?" he asked.

"Something is not forgotten just because no one speaks of it," replied Beatrice as she rearranged her dishevelled skirts. "We all know the signs: first the memory goes, then…"

"No, Beattie–!" Fosse slammed his metallic fist onto the seat. The letter fell to the floor.

"All that talk of Egyptian tombs and mummies and curses." She observed him from the corner of her eye. "Then you involved our son."

"Edward?" Fosse frowned. *But he wasn't there when the tomb was opened.*

"Our son is dead, Edgar." She avoided his gaze.

"But that was an accident! Not the–"

"And that Collins is to blame," she hissed.

"But he wasn't–" Fosse sat on the edge of the seat.

"He's the one who said Edward was well enough to travel. It's his fault. He took our child from us, Edgar." Beatrice unclipped her bag and fished out a handkerchief. "And she told him to! And now they are to be married. He'll have his own child though he robbed me of mine." She buried her head in her hands. "What are you going to do about it?"

Fosse blinked. His heart pounded in time with the clicking of his fingers.

"They are part of the curse?"

"Don't you see? Doctor Stewart and Doctor Collins, they are co-conspirators."

Silk of lapis blue? The eye patch? She is an agent of Horus.

"Yes, the one-eyed daemon and her mate?" Fosse slid back into the coach seat. *It is retribution for disturbing the princess, for defiling her resting place with Mr Umber's body.*

"Yes, yes. They will be our downfall." Beatrice nodded and wrung her handkerchief.

"That Stewart woman does well to hide her true nature," he said.

"But the patch gives her away. She can't hide her true face. Does she think me a simpleton?" His trembling fingers burrowed into the seat leather.

"Something must be done. We can't let them destroy you." Beatrice neatly folded her handkerchief and sighed. "I'll visit Doctor Stewart tomorrow. It's the maid's day off. She'll be alone for hours." She slipped the bundle into her bag and snapped the clasp shut. "I'll find out what they know."

Fosse snapped to attention.

"Be careful, Beattie." A shudder rolled up Fosse's arm; his flesh hand quivered in sympathy. "You can't trust her." His breathing, now shallow, joined the chorus.

"Be careful yourself, Edgar. All this talk of gods and curses and murder? If they hear you, Doctor Collins will send you to the madhouse. You'll end up in Bedlam, in a cell next to your uncle. What would I do then? You are the last of your line." Beatrice twirled her hair and pouted. "I should be all alone. And penniless."

Dearest Beattie. He gazed into her dark eyes. *You're the only one who understands me.*

"Never fear, my love. You are provided for," he said.

"I never doubted you, my dear." Beatrice eyed him as she patted his chest where the amulet lay under his pin-tucked linen shirt. It warmed at her touch.

"It will all work out. Trust me." Beatrice kissed his flesh hand. "I have everything under control."

Chapter 3: Retribution

A flustered ruckus rolled down the hallway and thumped on the parlour door. Viola closed the Egyptology book, slipped it behind the cushions on the couch and tugged at her collar, fumbling with the diminutive mother-of-pearl buttons at her neck.

Polly entered and cleared her throat. She clutched her printed-paisley shawl as she bobbed, barely managing to announce the new arrival before Mrs Fosse scuttled through the door. A beaked and feathered monstrosity jiggled atop Mrs Fosse's pristine coiffure. One long feather tapped her ruby-velveted shoulder. Her hand gripped her bulging carpet bag.

Such a spectacle - a jumble of couture, frivolity and practicality. Viola bit her tongue. She rose from her chair and stepped forward.

"Mrs Fosse? How lovely to see you again."

"Please, it's Beatrice. I shall answer to nothing else."

Viola ushered her to the over-stuffed chair next to the couch.

"Will you be staying for tea?" Polly pursed her lips and tucked her own bag under one arm.

"Ah, that would be splendid," replied Beatrice.

"Thank you, Polly," said Viola.

Polly straightened her bonnet and clicked the door shut behind her.

Viola's brow tightened. *Poor Polly, caught up on her afternoon off.*

"To what do I owe the pleasure, Beatrice?" asked Viola, as she tried to avoid the glassy-eyed stare of Beatrice's picture bonnet.

Beatrice sat on the edge of the chair, cupped Viola's chin in her hand and tsked.

"Oh, my darling, are you unwell? You look so pale. Like you've seen a ghost." She glanced at the lumpy cushions on Viola's chair. "Mr Fosse said you're worried about a curse." She sighed. "You were warned about the mummy. But look, I brought something to cheer you up." She grasped the carpet bag in her hands. "A surprise gift for my dear new friend."

Viola sat down on the lounge, positioning her bustle so as not to dislodge the camouflage of cushions. She folded her hands in her lap and smiled sweetly.

Surprises never end well.

Beatrice's hand snaked into the tapestry bag, rummaged in its bottomless depths and pulled out a small wooden box.

"For you. A brand new set of pigments. I researched them in the *Artists Manual*. Only the best quality for my dear friend."

Viola unhooked the catch and opened the box. A colourful array of stamped cakes filled the bottom compartments. A dozen metal tubes sat in the compartments near the hinge. They were indeed top of the range. And expensive.

"I wasn't sure what you preferred, so I bought both," said Beatrice.

"A splendid gift, but you shouldn't have gone to such an expense."

"Nonsense." Beatrice leaned closer. "And I have an ulterior motive," she whispered.

Here it was. *Surprises always have a price.*

"You've gone pale again." Beatrice giggled. "Relax, Viola. It won't be your undoing."

The bird on Beatrice's bonnet wiggled. Viola examined a tube of Rose Madder and flipped it over in its compartment.

"My dear Viola, I've heard you are quite the artist and have painted portraits of local gentry." Beatrice scanned the parlour walls. "What a pity you don't have any of your own work on display."

"I leave that decision to others." Viola's cheeks burned.

"Yes, beauty is in the eye of the beholder, but I am told your work is absolutely unique."

"I'll take that as a compliment," replied Viola.

"As it was intended, my dear."

Viola shut the box of pigments and closed the latch.

"I would like to commission you to paint my portrait. I wish to give it to my Edgar, as an anniversary present." Beatrice clutched her carpet bag closer to her chest. "Please say yes. I am determined."

"But you haven't seen my work," said Viola.

"Ah, you have caught me out," replied Beatrice. "We had occasion to consult Sir Archibald Huntington-Smythe after Mr Fosse had a little…" Beatrice frowned, "…accident on a dig in Egypt."

"His hand?"

Beatrice nodded.

"The poor dear would die if he couldn't actually get his hands dirty when he is on a dig," replied Beatrice. "I saw Sir Archibald's portrait on the wall. Imagine my surprise to find out the painter was you, my new friend!" She leaned forward and grinned. "The pigments are a bribe, so I can see your studio. See where the artist works and perhaps view something in progress?"

The parlour door clicked open. The sweet smell of fresh Assam tea followed Polly through the parlour. Her shawl slipped down one arm as she placed the tea tray on the side table.

"If that is all, Miss?" Polly pulled the shawl over her shoulder and secured it under her arm.

"Yes, don't worry. We shall cope on our own, Polly."

"Thank you, Miss." Polly curtsied. "I'll be back by tea time. Doctor Collins is coming for supper."

Viola waited until the door clicked shut behind Polly.

"I do apologise," she said. "It's Polly's afternoon off."

"I didn't know." Beatrice shook her head, and grinned. She sprang to her feet and shoved her carpet bag onto her arm.

"The perfect opportunity to view your studio! Shall we?" Beatrice picked up the tea tray. "After you, my dear Viola."

The thick aroma of linseed oil and walnut greeted them. It enveloped the room - rich, smooth, pleasant. Viola took a deep breath. Her pulse slowed.

Almost as effective as a good cup of tea. She placed the paint box on a small table by the easel.

"Thank you again for the pigments."

"What are friends for if not to be of encouragement," replied Beatrice.

Cups rattled. Beatrice plopped the tray onto a trolley near the door, poured a cup of tea and offered it to Viola. Beatrice surveyed the studio, grinned and clapped her hands together.

"Oh, my!" Her heels tapped on the chequerboard-tiled floor as she sashayed to the covered easel in the centre of the room. "May I peek?"

Viola gulped down a mouthful of tea. Before she could reply, Beatrice whipped the canvas from the easel. A paintbrush clattered to the floor.

"How clumsy of me." Beatrice scooped up the brush, carpet bag swinging on her arm, and picked flecks of dry paint out of its bristles, as she peered at the portrait. An incomplete face floated in a sea of patched colour. A pair of piercing blue eyes stared back at them.

Viola snatched up the cloth and draped it back over the painting.

"Doctor Collins is a handsome man, is he not?" said Beatrice.

"It's not finished," replied Viola.

Beatrice sauntered over to the cluttered table nestled up against one wall. On it were scattered ceramic bowls, fluid filled jars, a mortar and pestle. A small chest of dishevelled square drawers sat on the table, some half-open, stuffed with rags and painting accoutrements. One drawer was filled with a forest of used paintbrushes. Beatrice slipped the brush into the copse of cream, red and black handles and examined the gallery of sketches pinned to the wall above the desk.

"Lovely. Do you have any finished paintings I can view?" she asked.

Viola nodded.

"Excellent. I'll pour more tea," said Beatrice.

Viola dragged open the curtains, revealing a wall of full-length windows, and lifted a long sheet off a row of canvases lined against the far wall. Their colours glowed in the afternoon sun.

"Exquisite." Beatrice's bonnet feathers brushed Viola's ear.

Viola jumped. *Strange, I didn't hear her boots.*

"My, you are skittish, Viola." Beatrice offered her another cup of tea. "There's nothing like a good cup of tea to calm the nerves."

Viola took a sip. She licked her lips. Sweet. She had forgotten how heavy-handed Beatrice was with sugar.

"That's what I tell Mr Fosse when he starts rambling on about his mummy and the curse." Beatrice smiled and tapped Viola's elbow lightly. "And him, a man of science."

Viola gulped another mouthful of tea. *Sickly sweet.* She coughed, struggling to swallow the hot liquid.

"Curse?" she asked.

"It's silly. He's so superstitious." She leaned closer and whispered. "He wears a protective amulet, you know. Always. He thinks I don't know."

"What does it look like?"

"Hmmm?"

"The amulet?" asked Viola.

"Oh," Beatrice waved her hand in the air, "some sort of eye. I thought it was part of his spiritualist group, but it looked like the one on that mummy coffin, the one he brought back from his last dig. Princess something-or-other."

"Princess Mehytenweskhet?"

"I think that's the one." Beatrice's eyes widened. "My, you pronounced that well. Are you sure you don't have some Egyptian blood in you?"

Beatrice finished her tea and clunked her cup onto the table. She flipped up some sketches and peered at the layer of drawings underneath.

"I do like this one. Sir Archibald, isn't it?" she asked.

Viola wiped her forehead. *That tea was hot.* She stepped out of the sunlight and squinted.

"Do you paint at all, Beatrice?"

"I dabble in a lot of things." Beatrice's voice was muffled. Drawers rattled. A distant buzzing circled the room. "But they say art bares the soul. I don't think I am ready to expose my daemons to the world. You're much braver than I, Viola."

Daemons?

Jars clinked. Something cracked. The sharp smell of turpentine engulfed Viola. A wave of nausea followed.

Beatrice turned in a flurry of ruby silk. Searing sunlight glared off a golden amulet at her throat and clawed at Viola's eye.

Viola stumbled toward the windows. She gasped for fresh air. Pain consumed her ocular cavity. She grabbed at the eye to block out the light, flailed blindly at the curtains and wrenched them shut.

Light seeped through the chintz. Streams of dust danced between the shadows.

"Is there something wrong?" Beatrice grabbed Viola's wrist.

A powerful, intoxicating bouquet clung to her; sickly sweet with a hint of geranium… and a bitter edge.

That smell.

Beatrice's face smudged, like thinners on oil paint; it melted into the aromatic fumes and rose, like flames, around her.

Viola's body shuddered. Acid rose up her oesophagus. Her head spun out of control. The buzzing swarmed, drowning out Beatrice's voice. Viola felt her body list to one side. She flung out her hand, groping for anything to steady herself. Her fingers wrapped around a thin handle. The easel toppled and clattered dully to the floor.

Shadows peeled off the walls, oozed out of the portraits and swirled around the room. They clutched at Viola's sleeves and skirt. Portraits growled behind her.

Cool liquid trickled along her thumb and dripped from the paintbrush in her hand. Each plop echoed in her head.

Viola turned to Beatrice for assistance. Beatrice was motionless. Her ruby skirts swelled and fluttered in the breeze-less room. They licked the floor, consumed Beatrice's body and engulfed her face.

Blazing red eyes glared back at Viola - red and fierce as fire. They moved closer, in a silken inferno. The growling grew louder. A sharp, spicy, decadent aroma followed, tickled her nose and clawed at her throat.

Plumes of silk twisted around Viola's waist. Others forged a feline shape. Ears, muzzle and mouth formed around the scalding ruby-red eyes. The room roared.

Beatrice was gone.

Viola tugged at her bindings. They cinched, securing their grip. Silk manacles throbbed around her wrist and yanked her toward the nightmare before her.

Closer.

Head of lion. Skin of woman. No, that's impossible!

Viola gripped the paintbrush and stabbed at the creature.

"You don't exist. You're not real. The curse is not real!"

Closer.

Its mouth opened.

Closer.

Scorching breath rushed over Viola's skin. The maw widened until the room was consumed in darkness and flame.

The smell of fresh oils saturated the studio. The sharp tang of turpentine hovered at the edges. It permeated into Henry's clothing and tickled his brain. He shook his head and inched his way through the remains of broken glass and shredded canvases toward the windows, in his search for fresh air.

Henry surveyed the disorder. Frayed canvases lay partially hidden under a shredded drop cloth. Soiled brushes sprinkled the floor. Paint stains trailed back to the work table where upended jars spilled their liquid over the tabletop. Blood red paint flooded the exposed drawers, dripped onto the floor and oozed along the edges of the tiles.

Viola's easel teetered in the far corner, balanced on a discarded pile of paintings. A wet canvas clung to the easel frame. Frenzied brush strokes scored the canvas surface: smudged blacks, browns and yellows. Jagged edges coalesced, a mask of a lioness barely recognisable in the chaos.

Henry stared at the canvas. Red eyes glared back at him, accusing him: *You should have listened.* They followed him as he circled the room towards the painting.

A furrow deepened in his forehead. He ran his hand over his moustache. *Viola, what have you done?* He closed his eyes and took a deep breath. It caught in his throat. Something very unpleasant knocked at his consciousness. Henry swallowed. He refused to let it in, willed it to leave. He wiped a tear from the corner of one eye. How could she have done such a thing?

How did I miss the signs? If word got out… If the Constables had been called…

I'm sorry, Viola. Henry's fingernails bit into his palm. *You will not be sent to Bedlam. I'll protect you. At any costs.*

China crunched behind him. Henry jerked his head in Polly's direction and sucked in his breath.

Polly picked her way through the debris and hovered beside Henry, sneaking glances at the canvas out of the corner of her eye.

"Viola?" he asked as he started toward the door.

Polly held out her hand, gesturing him to stop.

Henry let out a long breath. "How is she?"

"She's resting." Polly bowed her head. "I've locked the door, sir. For her own safety." She dropped a key into Henry's hand. "I hope I've done the right thing."

"I think that's for the best." Henry nodded and pocketed the key. He tried to banish the image of his dear Viola caged like a mad… His fingernails dug deeper into his palm. Viola was *not* mad. There must be an explanation. And he would find one.

Another long, deep breath.

"And Mrs Fosse?" he asked.

"She's nowhere to be found, sir." Polly wrung the corner of her apron. "Um, there's blood, sir."

Henry looked Polly in the eye, trying not to give himself away. His forehead tightened.

"Near the tea tray." Polly frowned and pointed toward the table.

China skittered under Henry's feet as he strode to the upturned tray near the table. An intoxicating floral perfume erupted around him. Euphoric. His muscles relaxed. His head whirled.

Henry staggered back from the fumes, shook his head and eyed the broken crockery through narrowed lids.

Since there's no such thing as curses… Henry whipped a handkerchief from his pocket, picked up a teacup remnant with the tips of his fingers and inhaled. A heady floral scent masked a faint bitter odour. Henry's moustache twitched. Something familiar… but…

"Poison!" Henry's heart pounded.

"Poison?" echoed Polly.

"Then Miss Viola's not going mad?" The corner of her apron fell from her fingers. "Someone is doing this to her?"

Henry nodded. *Nothing supernatural about it.* His chest muscles relaxed. He could save Viola; this is what he was trained for. *But which poison?* His mind raced. *I need facts.*

"Symptoms–" He turned to Polly. "What are her symptoms?"

"Her skin is all red and she seems to have a temperature." Polly stuttered, as she approached Henry. "She's thirsty and–"

"Mad as a hatter!"

"But I thought–" said Polly, as she fidgeted with her apron.

"It's a mnemonic we learned at University: 'Mad as a hatter. Red as a beet. Dry as a bone.'" Atropine poisoning! He wrapped the cup piece in the handkerchief, shoved it in his pocket, and started for the door. "Look after her, Polly. I'll be back in an hour. I need to fetch some more medicines. I need–"

Pilocarpine. Henry froze mid-step. *Viola has some in her clinic. Excellent. But there was something else as well…*

Henry pulled out the wrapped cup remnant and thrust it in Polly's direction.

"Smell this. Do you recognise anything?" he asked.

Polly sniffed the bundle and wrinkled her nose. Her eyes widened.

"There *was* something. That flowery smell. In Miss Viola's bedroom when the gaslight went out. I thought I was imagining it."

"Do you recognise it?"

Polly shook her head.

Henry's shoulders slumped.

"Watch your mistress. Any new symptoms could be important." Henry's mouth hardened. *There must be something I'm missing.*

Henry slouched in his chair, and leaned his elbow on the windowsill. It had been a long day, touch and go for the first several hours. Finally Viola was resting, her fingers entangled in her dark auburn curls on the pillow. Henry took a deep breath.

Thank God. He dragged his gaze from the sleeping Viola, rubbed his eyes and stared out the bedroom window.

Lamplighters were making their way along Greater Marylebone Street. Their muted footsteps marked time with the wall clock.

He silently counted the beats:

One. Two. Three. Four.

Breathe.

One. Two. Three. Four.

Breathe.

He must remain calm, must keep his wits about him, must be ready when Viola awoke, or he would be of no use. Until then, all he could do was wait.

Henry ran his hand over his moustache. Chin bristles scratched his fingertips. He'd send for his shaving kit when she was out of danger. It wouldn't do to look dishevelled. Viola would only fuss and he didn't want to cause her more grief.

The lamplighter's wooden ladder clattered against the pole below the bedroom window. He clambered half way up, opened a glass pane, wiped it down and lit the flame. The lamp burst into life, its parchment coloured glow a sentry against the oncoming darkness. The lamplighter shimmied back down, unhooked the ladder and tramped to the next pole, and the next. A chain of reassuring pools of light followed in his wake.

A faint click broke Henry's trance. The bedroom wall lamps flickered in the draft.

"You shouldn't sit in the dark, sir," said Polly. She glanced at his creased coat slung over the end of the bed, then back to him. She bit her lip.

Henry examined his attire. His crumpled shirt sleeves were scrunched above his elbows, his waistcoat was twisted. His abandoned starched-linen collar lay on the dressing table, next to the untouched luncheon tray, a wooden-tube stethoscope and a used syringe in a kidney dish. Henry rolled down his sleeves, adjusted his shirt and fastened the buttons of his waistcoat.

"I've pigeon pie and fried mushrooms." Polly presented a supper tray with two covered plates, teapot, cup and saucer.

"I'm not hungry," said Henry. He frowned as he turned to Polly. "I apologise, Polly."

Polly nudged Henry's collar to one side, settled the supper tray on the dressing table, and frowned.

"You missed luncheon, sir. You need to eat something. You'll be no good to Miss Viola if you can't concentrate." She lifted the lid off the plate. The buttery aroma of fresh pastry and earthy smell of mushrooms snared Henry's attention.

Fried mushrooms are Viola's favourite. He glanced at Viola, sleeping peacefully.

A smile flickered over Henry's lip. He straightened his shoulders, picked up the fork and poked a steaming mushroom.

Polly crossed to Viola's bed.

"Miss Blake has enquired what should she tell the patients."

"I expect to see an improvement tomorrow." Henry's fork tinked on the plate. "Tell Miss Blake to inform them she has a touch of cold and to reschedule their appointments for next week."

Polly nodded as she rearranged the pillows and tucked a loose sheet

under the mattress. Viola murmured; her hand twitched on the pillow.

Henry leaped to his feet, snatched up his stethoscope. Polly stepped out of the way, almost knocking the night table, as he rushed to Viola's side. He placed the wooden tube against Viola's chest, closed his eyes and swallowed. The heartbeat was steady, strong, no longer racing. He sighed, pulled his chair closer to the bed and slumped into it. *Normal.*

Polly fidgeted behind him.

"What's this doing here?" asked Polly.

"Hmm, what's that?" asked Henry, not taking his eyes from Viola.

"That Egyptology book." Polly picked up the book. "I returned it to the parlour."

A card fluttered to the floor. Henry bent over and retrieved it. Gilt edging glowed in the lamp light. *Doctor Viola Stewart is requested to attend the...*

"It's the invitation to the Museum's Egyptian Exhibit opening," said Henry.

"Oh, Miss Viola will be annoyed to miss it."

"I'll send her apologies," said Henry, "when I return that book."

Viola mumbled inaudibly. Henry leaned closer.

"... Must tell... Professor..." She rolled away and buried her head into the pillow.

"Tell him what?" Henry's moustache twitched. He placed one hand on Viola's forehead. *No fever.* He caressed her cheek. *You're safe now. Everything will be all right.* Viola's breathing settled into a regular rhythm.

"Is there anything I can do, sir?" asked Polly as she collected the luncheon tray.

"A light breakfast for your mistress, in the morning. Broth, I think," replied Henry.

"More water?" Polly hovered near the door. "More medicine? Shall I send for your man?"

Henry peered at Polly, through heavy lids, and smiled weakly.

"Some fresh clothes and my shaving kit would not go amiss. Thank you, Polly."

The door clicked shut. They were alone.

Henry clasped his hands around hers and kissed her fingers. His chin wrinkled. Tears blurred his vision.

Who would do this to you? He brushed his thumb over her hand and whispered in her ear: "I couldn't bear to lose you, Vi." He kissed her forehead and slumped in the chair, still clasping her hand.

Henry's eyelids fluttered. The house was quiet. Nothing stirred in the street. He concentrated on Viola's breathing. The wall clock kept time.

Tick tock. Growing more distant...

Tick tock. Slowing...

Tick...

Silence.

Crash!

Henry leaped to his feet and spun to face the door behind him. His fingers cramped as he clenched the stethoscope and brandished it before him.

"What the devil–?" Sunlight glared in his eyes through the window. He blinked, waiting for his eyes to adjust.

Polly stood in the doorway, crockery scattered at her feet, her mouth open in a silent scream. She stared, wide-eyed and pointed to the bed.

"Sir, she's–"

Henry's heart froze. Sheets trailed from the doorway, through scattered clothing toward the empty bed. His lungs refused to breathe.

Viola was gone.

The seat vibrated as the plectocycle trundled over the cobblestones. High wheels rattled on either side of Viola, dampening the rhythmic chugging of its small engine.

Footsteps clapped on the footpath. Viola's heart pounded.

She eased back on the steering levers. The plectocycle slowed. Steam rose, engulfed the contraption and warmed her ears. The engine decelerated. Viola twisted to glance over her shoulder and peered along Greater Marylebone Road. Long shadows slithered along the footpath inching toward the lamplight.

She strained to listen.

Nothing.

The engine sputtered and coughed. A puff of smoke belched. Pain pricked Viola's eye. She wiped away tears with the back of her hand, trying not to rub grit into her eye.

Red brick townhouses loomed before her as she entered High Street. Their sombre chimneys twitched along the skyline, listening to her every move. Dark windows glared back with their blank eyes. Unblinking.

They whispered: *Cursed.*

More footsteps echoed behind her.

Viola leaned forward on the levers, pushing the plectocycle faster; the swinging lantern above the front wheel her only guide.

Blood thumped through her chest and in her ears. She struggled to breathe as another wave of heat flashed over her body.

She kicked the pedal and thrust the lever forward, spinning her contraption northward along High Street.

The footsteps quickened, keeping pace as she sped away from her unseen pursuer. She glanced over her shoulder. A shadow peeked over the roof. It crept across the windows and crawled down the wall, oozing onto the cobblestones, edging nearer.

Viola shuddered. Her hand jerked. The wheels squealed, sending the plectocycle up a side lane past The Queen's Head.

A gust pressed at her back, ramming rain drops down her collar and propelling her ever forward. Wisps of hair whipped at her eye, snaked into her mouth. Smoke breathed down her neck and fingered her nostrils. Acrid. Hot. Like brimstone.

Tenements crowded closer. Shadows swayed and licked the remaining patch of sky between the huddled walls. The lane narrowed, funnelling Viola toward a skeletal iron gate, its bones barely visible in the darkness.

Paddington Street Gardens. Viola swallowed. Her gaze tracked the brick wall; curved shadows peeked above the top course. *Saint George's cemetery. No time to turn up the lantern. What good would it do?* Beatrice was devoured by a creature of fire and shadows. Viola shuddered, remembering its growl. *The flame would attract the beast.* She glanced around her, searching the dark. The shadows were everywhere, waiting for her to lose her concentration so they could devour her as well.

She forced the levers further forward. The plectocycle jerked and scraped, pulling to the right.

Botheration. Viola eased off the left lever and eyed the darkened alley ahead. *Room enough for a bicycle, but the plectocycle?*

The gate rattled, cautioning her as she entered the shadows. Viola flinched. The gate moaned. She pulled back on the right lever and turned into the blackness, following the walled edge of the gardens.

A glimmer of light flickered ahead. Branches trembled above her, depositing chilled beads of rain on her face. Metal scraped the brick wall as she sped toward her goal - the lone street lamp at the end of the dark.

Flecks of debris spat at Viola's cheeks. Her hand twitched. There wasn't time to compress the axle width. She dare not slow down, dare not let the shadows catch her. Would it even work while the plectocycle was in motion? No. The street lamp was her only hope.

The welcoming glow of the street lamp expanded until it spilled into the laneway. Viola halted in the pool of light, almost hugging the lamp post. Sweat beaded on Viola's forehead, along the edge of her eyepatch and dribbled down her cheek. Her throat burned.

She wiped sweat from her forehead and glanced along the street. Pools of light dotted the footpath in both directions, spilling onto the cobblestones, forming rivulets of shadow. Glistening puddles lined the edge of the street, light and shadows shifting across the surface.

The moon's reflection shimmered in the puddle beside her, pushing back the patches of shadow that licked the edges of her sanctuary. Viola extinguished the cycle's lantern flame and sighed.

Safe for now. Safe from the flame. Safe from the shadows that pursued it, like a moth to the flame.

A rivulet of water crept under Viola's collar and trickled down her spine. A shiver fluttered over her skin.

Botheration.

She reached toward the box behind her and pressed a button. The lid popped open. With a whir and a rattle, a metal frame telescoped from the box. A canvas canopy unfurled. Tassels trembled as the final rod clicked in place.

Rain thumped softly on the canvas, drizzled off its edges and tinked onto the lantern, forming a protective cage of water. The Professor's house was not far. Viola had to warn him of the danger. And tell him the sad news about Beatrice.

Droplets of water dribbled off the portico and plopped on the tessellated tiles beneath Viola's feet. The maid remained in the doorway, eyeing Viola down her aquiline nose.

"I need to see Professor Fosse," pleaded Viola.

"It's very late," said the maid.

"I apologise, but it's an urgent matter." Viola shook beads of water off her glove and fumbled in her pocket. "It's imperative I see him." She shoved a soggy introduction card in the direction of the maid.

The maid held the corner of the card and grimaced as she peered at the smudged print.

"Wait here." Her voice was clipped, her thin lips pursed.

The door clicked shut.

Viola rested one hand on the door. *The Professor needed to know about Beatrice.* She huddled close to the portico lamp, cringing from the shadows beyond the veil of water. *He needed to know about the beasts in the shadows.*

Hooves splashed in the distance. A faint growl lingered on the breeze.

That was close. Too close. Viola pulled her plectocycle up onto the final step and held her breath. She was exposed out here. She needed to be inside.

What's taking that maid so long?

The door creaked open several inches. Viola's grip tightened on the plectocycle.

The maid's brow creased.

"Professor Fosse will see you," she said.

Viola's hands relaxed. She pressed a button on the decorated backrest. The canopy folded back onto itself, the frame jittered and retracted and slid back home. She slipped one hand behind the contraption's seat and yanked on the lever. Steam hissed. Gears whirred as the back axle telescoped inward until the wheels nudged the engine box.

"You can't bring that… contraption in here," grumbled the maid. "I don't care who you are."

"I can't leave such a valuable machine on the street." Viola straightened her shoulders and looked the maid in the eye. "I'm sure Professor Fosse will not be pleased if his guest is robbed outside his very house."

"Very well–" The maid huffed. "But only in the hall." She eyed

Viola up and down. "Doctor, you say? I suppose you're one of those Museum types?" She turned her back on Viola, opened the door wider and glanced over her shoulder. "I won't have anyone riding contraptions around my house."

Viola lifted the cycle over the threshold and rolled it into the well-lit hallway.

The maid eyed the growing puddle, glared at Viola and pushed the door shut.

"He'll see you in the study." She waved her hand in the direction of the nearby doorway and strode down the hall.

The sarcophagus standing sentry at the door stared at Viola as if it knew something.

Cursed, it whispered.

Its raised eyebrow reminded her of Henry – and his soft, reassuring voice: *Curses aren't real.*

The sarcophagus' mouth curled at one corner.

"Disturbing, isn't it?" Fosse's voice was slow, his attention still fixed on his papers. "It's always watching."

Viola bit her lip and turned to face Fosse. She flicked another drop of water from her gloves, trying to ignore the sarcophagus' smug stare.

Fosse sat at his desk, peering through a pair of mag-specs at an array of inked papyri. He twiddled a dial on the rim; a tinted lens clicked in place. He mumbled to himself as he plopped one… three… five cubes of sugar into a teacup on the tray on his desk.

Viola cleared her throat and stepped closer to the desk.

"Professor, I have some terrible news." Viola bowed her head. "I'm sorry. I didn't–"

Fosse glanced up from his papers; his expressionless dark eyes peered through her.

Perhaps he already knows?

"Then we'll need a cup of tea first." He poured Viola a cup of tea, plopped four sugar cubes into the liquid and stirred.

"Strong, sweet tea is always recommended for bad news." His smile mirrored that of his sentry-sarcophagus as he offered Viola the cup.

Steam rose from the golden liquid. Sweet perfume filled Viola's nostrils.

"Is this your special blend?" she asked.

Fosse gulped down a mouthful.

"You have a good nose," he replied. There was a definite slur in his speech. He blinked slowly and took another sip.

The poor man. One doesn't ordinarily show up, late at night, uninvited and announce 'your wife is dead'. It just isn't done in polite society. Despite Fosse's discourteous behaviour at the Museum, he deserved to have the news broken to him gently.

Viola nodded slowly and took a sip of sweet tea. Warmth radiated through her chest, into her shoulders, loosening her muscles.

But how to tell him?

She drifted over to the mantelpiece. A silver frame glinted in the firelight. She examined the photograph: a happy family – Beatrice, Fosse and a pale young man standing in front of pyramids.

Beatrice wore a crisp white pinafore, seemingly untouched by the desert heat. Her eyes looked away from the camera, toward the two men beside her.

Fosse grinned under his pith helmet, a monstrous pick slung over his shoulder. His other hand rested on the young man's shoulder.

Viola squinted at the tintype, struggling to focus. Fosse wore no gloves; both hands were flesh. The photograph must've been taken before the accident.

The young man's thin face peeked out from under a sun hat. *I wonder who he is?*

She glanced at the statuettes on either side of the frame. Her hand trembled. One had the head of a falcon, the other the head of a lioness.

Horus and Bast. A hot flush swept over Viola.

"You–" Her throat was parched. She licked her dry lips.

"Drink your tea, Doctor Stewart," slurred Fosse. "You'll feel much better."

The floral bouquet wafted around her face – warm and inviting.

Just one more sip.

Viola raised her cup. Something tugged at her mind. She glanced back at the photograph. Her arm froze.

"Is that a nurses' uniform?" asked Viola.

"…yes." The reply was slow. "Nurse Beatrice." Fosse sighed. "We met at the Cairo hospital. Beattie worked in the Pharmacy and helped with surgery. Beauty and brains." Fosse slurped his tea and smiled.

"And the young man?" Viola rested her cup back into the saucer. Something squirmed in her mind.

"Our son." Beatrice's voice was clear and crisp.

Viola's cup rattled on the saucer. Hot liquid cascaded over the rim and drenched her finger. Pain seared along her arm.

"You're alive!" Viola's grip loosened. The saucer shattered on the hearth. The cup followed. Scorching tea seeped into Viola's skirt and sloshed over the floor.

"Oh, dear." Fosse didn't flinch.

"Let me help you with that, my dear." Beatrice strode towards Viola; her boot crunched the ceramic shards. She grabbed Viola's hand and rolled it over.

"Beattie…" Fosse's metal fingers clicked on the table. "I'm sorry."

"Drink your tea, Edgar. I'll fix it. Like I always do."

Fosse nodded and drank his tea.

Beatrice's cold gaze held Viola. Her mouth froze in a determined, unnerving smile.

Viola swallowed. She had misjudged Beatrice. This was no flighty female only interested in gossip and gardening. That was a ruse, a camouflage for the calculating woman now before her, a woman in complete control of her emotions, her husband's fate – and hers.

Beatrice smirked and gripped Viola's wrist tighter.

Pipes clunked near the windows. Water sprayed in the terrariums, cascading down the glass. A heady sweet, floral scent lifted into the air. A familiar smell...

Viola's eyes widened. The smell of Beatrice's perfume. The smell of... the tea Beatrice poured for her on their meeting, the tea Fosse had poured for her, the tea that drenched her clothing.

Botheration.

"Drugs are wondrous things, my dear." Beatrice stroked Viola's hair. "They can heal, reduce pain… cause hallucinations." She glanced at her husband. "And cloud thoughts, making one easily controlled."

She twisted Viola's arm.

"I see you didn't drink all of your tea, my dear Viola. Not to worry." Beatrice delved into her pocket and pulled out a large syringe. She squeezed the plunger. Liquid oozed from the needle tip. Drops trickled down its shaft into the puddle of tea on the floor. "I'm always prepared for life's little surprises."

She plunged the needle into Viola's arm. Searing heat shot along her veins, tracked up her arm and flooded her chest. Viola slumped forward.

Beatrice's arms wrapped around her, pulling her closer toward her chest, toward a medallion. Toward the Eye of Ra. Hot metal pressed into Viola's cheek. Blood thumped in her veins, rushed through her neck. She fought to keep her eye open.

The thumping slowed… fading into silent darkness.

The sharp stench of sulphur pricked at Viola's nostrils. Her head throbbed as several swarms of bees assaulted her brain, insisting on finding their own means of escape. Machinery chugged in the distance, belching out whiffs of oil and grease with each hiss. Something scuffled in the darkness. Muffled voices murmured around her. Unintelligible.

Viola cracked open an eyelid. Blackness engulfed her. Lamplight flickered over the top of the dark rim surrounding her, a couple feet above where she lay. A metal strut stood at each corner of the rim, forming a scaffold. A rectangular stone hovered several feet in the air, suspended by wires and chains.

She struggled to sit up. Tight restraints dug into her wrists and tugged at the lacing of her boots. She rolled onto her side, knocking her elbow on something solid. Dust wafted up her nose, mixed with a faint, syrupy smell of resin.

The murmuring ceased.

Her fingers walked along the cold stone prison around her.

A sarcophagus? A shiver ran up her spine. What had she gotten herself into this time?

Footsteps approached. A shadow moved into the rectangle border of light above her.

"Mise ielle!" Beatrice's face loomed above her. She snatched a lamp from an assistant's hand. In its light, she looked exotic and almost unrecognisable; her hair was pulled back into a severe braid, her eyes rimmed with thick kohl and her lips painted. A collar of shimmering gold, embellished with black glass and red jasper covered her shoulders. Fine, red linen robes fluttered as she moved, showing off her bare arms and accentuating her olive skin. The cloying reek of resin wafted around her head.

"Beatrice?"

"You're awake. How unfortunate for you." Beatrice's eyes narrowed. "It is forever scribed, 'For he who shall lay a finger on my family, he shall have no heir, his beloved shall be taken away before his face. *Her* tomb shall not exist in the necropolis, *her* corpse shall not be to the ground, and his heart shall not be content in life.'" Her mouth curled at one corner. "Retribution will be mine, my dear."

Beatrice spun on her heel and fluttered out of sight, no doubt bent on preparing for her retribution. Viola lifted her shoulders, trying to raise herself high enough to glimpse beyond the sarcophagus.

"How much longer?" Beatrice's accented voice was hard.

"Half an hour." The man's voice oozed charm, reminding Viola of the lanky Egyptian with the snake-oiled grin. *Mr Chartha?* She slumped to the floor. *He was in on it all along.*

A burst of heat rolled over the sarcophagus, followed by a strong smell of resin and bitter perfume. Metal clanked. Glass shattered. Chartha cursed. Beatrice chastised him.

Viola squirmed. *This was no imagined curse. This was real. Beatrice and Chartha meant her harm. Her heart pounded. I have to get out of here!* Her boots hammered against the stone.

"Don't tire yourself, my dear. No one can hear you down here." Beatrice laughed. Bottles clinked.

Viola's heart sank. *Calm.* She had to remain calm.

Concentrate. I need to escape. I've been in worse situations. What have I got to help? She clutched at her neck, curling her fingers around the oval pendant Sir Archibald had given her. She sighed. *Excellent, I still have my lock picks.* She patted her pockets and smiled. Beatrice hadn't searched her. She twisted her bound hands across her torso, bending as much as her corset would allow, reached her fingers into her skirt pocket and extricated her penny knife.

Now to just cut the–

The knife slipped from her fingers and clattered onto the stone base.

The bottles fell silent. Footsteps hurried toward her. Viola flipped out her skirts and shifted sideways onto the knife. The tip dug into her thigh.

She bit her lip, willing herself not to cry out.

"You should be in the nut house," hissed Beatrice as she waggled a dagger in the air.

"Why me?" asked Viola.

"Serendipity." Beatrice smirked. "Fortune favoured your fiancé when he so generously offered you his place of honour at the unwrapping. Not to worry. Fate provided me with a much more satisfying retribution." She toyed with the tip of her dagger and chuckled. "Oh, the ignominy that would have been Doctor Collins' when you were locked up in Bedlam. His fiancée, a mad woman! What else could he do? After all, Society must be protected. It's his duty."

"The curse? That was you?" asked Viola.

Beatrice nodded and waved the knife in Chartha's direction. The clinking resumed.

"It was an ingenious plan: first the apparition in the parlour." She widened her eyelids and placed her fingers on her mouth theatrically. "Oh, I *was* frightened. And then, plagued with horrendous visions, you attempted to end your own suffering by leaving the gas on." She shook her head and tsked. "Surely, a sign of a disturbed mind, full of guilt. And the daemon-painting? Obviously the frenzied madness of a deranged mind." Her voice remained calm. Cold.

"The French have an expression: *'jamais deux sans trois'*. Never twice without a third." Beatrice hurled the knife across the room. It clattered across the floor. She motioned to Chartha and leaned into the sarcophagus. His shadow fell over Viola's face as he grabbed her wrists and secured them. Beatrice's fingers tugged at Viola's collar. Cold crept down Viola's neck as Beatrice undid the buttons of Viola's bodice, down to her waist.

A thunderous clang rang through the room. Beatrice jerked her fingers away from Viola and spun toward the noise. The lamplight flickered.

"Go, see what that was," she said.

Chartha released Viola's wrists and padded off into the distance. Beatrice turned to Viola.

"You were supposed to be safely locked up, after I had informed the authorities you attacked me," spat Beatrice.

"But I didn't–"

Beatrice leaned closer. A heady floral scent followed her.

"Ah, but you did." She held one arm above the sarcophagus rim and pulled her jewelled collar low to reveal her collarbone. Long, bloody scratches tracked along her décolletage and down her forearm toward her wrist. "Or they would have believed so, if your precious Doctor Collins hadn't covered it up and told his Constabulary friends someone was trying to poison you." Spittle wet her lip. "They even assigned a constable to guard your house!"

Beatrice scraped her fingernails along the stone and hissed.

"Yet you are here. Declared the victim, not the attacker. Absolved of any and all crimes. You lead a charmed life, my dear. It pays to have the right friends."

"Now you will just have to disappear. 'Unable to endure the emotional upheaval of impending marriage, Viola Stewart flees London never to be seen again.' Just like her sister. Cowardice is obviously a family trait."

Viola's lungs seemed to collapse. She struggled to breathe. How did Beatrice know about Anne?

Beatrice eyed Viola, straightened her shoulders and grinned.

"I've read the letters," she said.

"How dare you!" Viola stomped her bound feet against the walls of the sarcophagus and yanked at the ropes around her wrists.

Beatrice licked her lips and ran a finger along the rim of the sarcophagus.

"How tragic when he finds a note from his beloved, declaring she can't live a lie..."

"He'll know it's not from me," said Viola.

Beatrice scoffed, snatched up papers and dangled them over Viola's face.

"I have samples of your writing and my dear brother is an excellent forger. So you see, my dear Viola, your Doctor Collins will have no choice but to believe his eyes."

Viola lunged her bound hands toward Beatrice, her fingers stretched, clawing in the direction of Beatrice's eyes.

"You bitch!"

Beatrice barely flinched, cocked her head and raised an eyebrow. Viola snarled and fell back onto the stone.

"And poor Viola, so distraught at her sister's disappearance, has forsaken her affianced to roam the world in a hopeless quest to find her beloved Anne." Beatrice took a deep breath and sighed. "So tragic. Doctor Collins will be heart-broken, pining for his lost love - again - having waited so very, very long." Her eyes narrowed. "He'll live the rest of his life wondering what he could have possibly done."

Beatrice grasped the edge of the stone sarcophagus and glared at Viola.

Viola twitched. Her fingers crept under the folds of her skirt, groping for the penny knife. She needed to distract Beatrice just a little longer…

"But why Henry? What did he ever do to you?" she asked.

"Your fiancé works in the Police morgue, doesn't he?" Beatrice scoffed. "How comforting it is to work with the dead. One's mistakes have fewer consequences."

Viola's fingers froze. She frowned. What sort of answer was that?

Beatrice sneered, turned and strode away in a flurry of red linen.

Rushed footsteps echoed and clattered into the room.

"They're here, Beattie." It was Professor Fosse. His voice was hushed and hurried. "That Doctor and some Constables."

"Professor?" asked Viola.

Fosse whimpered. *A chink in the armour? Perhaps she could make him see reason?*

"Please, help me! Beatrice is–"

"Don't be deceived, my love." Beatrice's voice trickled, as sweet as honey. "She wants to destroy you. She knows you killed them. She's the instrument of Horus and her minions have come for you."

"She's lying! I've no reason to hurt you. I tried to help you. Remember? When I thought Beatrice was dead. I tried to warn you of the–" Her fingers curled around the penny knife. She had to get away.

"See, Edgar, my love. Even now she weaves her lies to destroy us."

Silence.

"You know I'd never hurt you. Once she's destroyed, we will be free of her influence. All will be as it should be."

Fosse sniffled, mumbling a reply.

"Go, dearest. Make sure they won't find us."

His feet shuffled away.

"So, he did murder the Man in Grey and Mr Turner?" whispered Viola.

"Edgar?" Beatrice scoffed and turned away.

Viola palmed the knife behind her wrist.

"My snivelling wreck of a husband doesn't have the stomach for murder. I've always had to fix everything. Sweet young Turner helped rid me of Mr Umber, but he wanted more. He had to go." The corner of her mouth curled. "It was easy to make poor Edgar think he had murdered them."

Hollow footfalls approached the room. Beatrice had resumed preparations to seal Viola's fate. Viola hacked at the ropes on her wrist with the penny knife. The hemp cut into her flesh as she twisted her wrists.

Almost there...

She winced and held her breath, hoping Beatrice would ignore her.

The footsteps entered the room and stopped near Beatrice.

"The entry is secure." Chartha lowered his voice. "Your husband is skulking on the lower floor, muttering about Horus and jumping at shadows. They'll find him soon and Bedlam can have him."

"Excellent," whispered Beatrice.

Viola strained to overhear the conversation.

"How long must we wait to secure the inheritance?" he asked. "When can we return to Egypt?"

"I've told you." Beatrice's voice was clipped and harsh. "We're not returning to Egypt."

Crashing noises filtered into the room, as if funnelled along a shaft.

"What's that?" Beatrice hissed.

Chartha ran from the room. Viola held her breath, trying to listen for any sign of what was happening. Eventually, footsteps returned.

"He's come back." Chartha's voice faltered.

"The fool!" Metal clattered. Two sets of footsteps ran out of the room.

Viola's breathing raced. She heard nothing but the chug and hiss of steam. Perhaps she could free herself before they returned?

The penny knife cut through the last strand of rope. Viola sighed, pulled herself up and peeked over the edge of the sarcophagus. An overpowering, powdery aroma of frankincense slammed into her nostrils.

She coughed and scanned the room. Beatrice and Chartha were gone. Lamplight flickered over workbenches filled with glass bottles, metal bowls and rolled linen wrappings. Smoke danced across a vat of thick, unctuous resin simmering over an unattended brazier. A stack of crates lined the far wall.

Viola peered into the shadows. The only exit from the room was near one of the workbenches where Beatrice had deposited the letters, next to a portable *Moisture-Depleting Combustor Generator*. Either the Fosses had access to Mechanical Ownership and Operation Permits or someone had been pilfering equipment from the museum.

Viola's shoulders relaxed. She tugged at the taut rope around her boots, loosening the knot enough to wiggle her feet.

Muffled echoes syphoned down the tunnel. She glanced at the exit. It was empty. *For now.*

Viola kicked her feet and yanked at the rope.

The echoes grew louder. Faint voices whispered - too difficult to tell how close. There was no time to cut the ropes.

Viola snatched up her penny knife, sliced down her boot laces and wriggled her feet out of her boots. She climbed out of the sarcophagus, careful not to disturb the scaffolding, fetched one of the oil lamps and stuffed the letters into her pocket. Henry would never read such hurtful lies.

The stone floor chilled Viola's stockinged feet. Cold slithered up her calves. She padded along the corridor until she reached a branch in the tunnel. She lowered the lamp and hesitated; her leg ached, still biting from the nick from the penny knife.

How much further?

Muffled voices trickled down the tunnel ahead. Viola's heart pounded. She took a deep breath and pattered down the side tunnel, away from potential threat.

The tunnel ended at a locked door. Viola grinned, plucked two of the amethyst-headed picks from her pendant and pushed them into the lock. There was a satisfying click. She slipped the picks home and crept through the doorway.

A wall of crates blocked her path. Viola inched her way along the barricade and peeked around the last crate. It was an empty storeroom, full of crates and canvas covered treasures. Viola bit her lip. There was no time to gratify her curiosity.

She slipped through the room and followed a bricked corridor to an iron gate, bathed in sunlight. She peered through the bars. A set of stairs wound upward, encircling the Museum's brass and iron lattice-worked Ascension Chamber. Its glass casement gleamed in the morning light from the windows lining the Chamber shaft.

A faint shriek reverberated along the corridor behind her.

Botheration. Beatrice must have discovered I've escaped. Viola's heart raced. She fumbled with her lock picks, wrenched open the grate, slammed it behind her and snapped the lock shut.

She turned to the steps. How far under the museum was she? How many floors would she have to climb? The muscle of her leg burned. She ran her hand over her thigh. Traces of fresh blood smeared her palm. The penny knife must have cut worse than she'd thought.

Faced with the dreaded Ascension Chamber as her best means of escape, Viola froze. She could feel the blood thumping through her veins.

Courage, Viola. She took a deep breath and wrapped her fingers around the iron grate of the Chamber's door.

Footsteps thudded closer. She could hear Beatrice cursing, the words almost unintelligible with their venom. There was no choice. She wrenched open the doors and stepped into the Chamber.

Beatrice appeared at the iron gate, reached through the bars and lashed out in Viola's direction. Her caterwauling screeched through Viola's head.

Viola fumbled with her pendant, trying to replace the lock picks, as she stumbled back into the corner of the Chamber and thrust the lever upward. The cage shuddered and rose up into the light.

The Ascension Chamber rattled up toward the ground floor. Viola peered through the Chamber's glass walls at the papyrus documents, which lined the shaft. They told stories about death and the afterlife. She wasn't ready to join them yet. Her fingers trembled as they wrapped around the lever. She had heard the iron gate slam open, heard boots slapping on the stairs.

Too close.

The Ascension Chamber reached the first floor. Still the footsteps followed.

Calm. Viola counted her breaths as the Ascension Chamber continued upward. Each was longer than the last. The Chamber slowed and halted inside a claustrophobic brick room. A single oak door, with a wheel lock, was its only feature.

Viola squeezed through the Chamber's half-opened grate. The door was her only escape. She spun the wheel, threw open the door and ran out into piercing sunlight.

Sandy gravel pricked at the soles of her feet. She picked her way along the roof, trying to find smooth patches. Wind whisked around her ankles, bringing with it the faint clop of horse hooves from the street below. It played with her skirts and tugged at her hair.

The oak door slammed behind her. Viola spun to face the noise, grimacing as her feet scraped the roof's rough surface.

Beatrice shrieked and pounced on Viola.

"You shouldn't be here!" screamed Beatrice. "You should be part of the new display, your rotting corpse festering in Princess Mehytenweskhet's sarcophagus in full view of the museum's cursed mummy - my dear son."

She clawed at Viola's eye. The eye patch fluttered onto the roof.

"You're mad!" Viola twisted out of Beatrice's reach.

"Your precious Henry will not have you!" Beatrice sneered. She grabbed at Viola's bodice, catching the collar, and dragged her toward the edge of the roof.

Viola dug her feet into the surface, snagging her stockings on the gravel. She winced as she elbowed Beatrice in the chest, twisted her body and slumped to the ground. She lifted her knees and shoved her feet into Beatrice's stomach.

Buttons popped off Viola's bodice. Material ripped and loosened. Beatrice lost her balance. Her eyes widened as she stumbled backward, Viola's bodice still gripped in one hand. She stepped into the air and screamed as she plummeted off the edge of the roof.

"Beattie!" A flash of cream-coloured linen barrelled past Viola. "No!" The howl caught up in the breeze and slammed into Viola's eardrums. Fosse paused near the edge of the roof and wailed, edging closer with each cry.

Viola struggled to her feet and brushed shards of stone from her hands. Fresh beads of blood seeped from her palms. She eyed Fosse as he leaned forward to search the ground below. His straw hat fluttered in an errant updraught. His hand clenched. The mechanical hand whirred and whined. Blood dripped from his flesh one.

"Professor Fosse, please come away from the edge," Viola's heart raced. She inched closer to him, wincing with each step.

Fosse didn't respond. He stared at the ground, his body inclining further over the edge with each heartbeat. A wind flurry caught his straw hat, whisked it into the air and dumped it to the ground where Beatrice had fallen.

His hands relaxed. He lifted one foot and stepped forward.

"No, don't!" Viola lunged toward him, grabbed his flesh hand and threw herself backward, using all of her weight to pull him away from the precipice.

Fosse crumpled onto the roof and sobbed. Vacant eyes glanced through her; their gaze flitted over the roof. Viola crawled closer to him. *Just stay where you are.*

A flicker of blue ribbon caught her eye. Her eye patch wobbled in the breeze, caught on an uneven remnant of stone. Viola chuckled and seized the floundering fancy.

Wood scraped behind her. The door banged. *Chartha?* Viola sprang to her feet and turned to face another onslaught. A tall figure, with worried eyes and an immaculate waistcoat, strode toward her.

"Henry!" She rushed to him, ignoring the pain in her leg and burning soles of her feet.

Henry wrapped his arms around her and kissed her. She closed her eyes and breathed in his soothing scent - vanilla, spices and leather. Her shoulders relaxed.

"Thank God you're alive, Vi," he whispered, as he pulled back slowly, gathered her hands in his, and examined them. He sucked in a sharp breath.

"You're hurt?" he asked quietly.

Viola shrugged.

He untangled the ribbon from her fingers, placed the silk patch over her eye socket and secured the ties.

"How did you find me?" she asked.

"We found a trail of blood." Henry examined her hands and arms. "Are you sure you are all right?" he asked.

Viola frowned. Henry took a deep breath and continued:

"The trail led to the Ascension Chamber. And I know how much you hate them…"

"Then how did you know–?"

"I found this on the Chamber floor." He placed one of her amethyst-headed lock picks in her hand. "We kept looking till we found the trail again." His moustache twitched. "Viola, I thought–" He embraced Viola, buried his face in her hair and squeezed gently.

"Ahem." Constable Jones cleared his throat. "Sir?"

Henry glanced at Jones.

"They have the Egyptian in custody, sir. Perhaps Doctor Stewart would prefer to–" said Jones, avoiding Viola's direct gaze.

Viola nudged Henry and withdrew to a more appropriate distance. She glanced at her attire: no bodice, soiled chemise and corset cover, tattered skirts tucked into her waistband, and shredded stockings. *No wonder Jones' face is red.*

Creases formed at the edges of Henry's eyes as he removed his frock coat and offered it to Viola. She unhitched her skirts, slipped on the frock coat and tugged it tight.

Gravel crunched behind them.

"Professor Fosse?" Viola had almost forgotten about him.

Fosse rambled as he stumbled back toward the edge of the roof. Jones dashed after him.

"He tried to jump," She tugged Henry's arm. "To follow Beatrice."

"She–?"

Viola swallowed, lowered her gaze and nodded.

Jones seized Fosse and wrenched him back toward the door.

"Be gentle with him, Constable Jones," said Viola.

"But he's murdered two men and tried to do the same to you, Doctor Stewart." Jones unhooked handcuffs from his belt.

"No, it was Beatrice, Mrs Fosse. She drugged the professor and incriminated him for the murders." Viola shook her head as she hobbled to the edge. "She tried to kill me, too."

She peered over the edge. Beatrice's crumpled body lay on the blood-soaked ground, entangled in a whirlwind of crimson cloth.

Viola's head whirled. *It could've been me.* Her stomach churned. The ground spun. Henry's arm slipped around her waist and eased her close, warming her body and taking the weight off her throbbing feet. He led her back toward the Ascension Chamber.

"Where shall I take him, sir? Shall I arrest him?" asked Jones. "It's not safe to take him home."

"No." Henry's moustache twitched. "Take the poor fellow to Bethlem Royal Hospital. He'll be looked after."

Consigned to Bedlam. Viola hugged Henry. She glanced back over her shoulder. His fate could have easily been hers, if Henry hadn't realised she, too, was being drugged… *If he hadn't intervened…*

"Thank you," she whispered.

Alarm bells clanged below. Iron wheels clattered on the cobblestones. Puffs of grey smoke belched above the rooftop. Voices shouted and muttered.

Fosse wailed.

A breeze wafted around Viola's bare feet, chilling her ankles.

"I don't suppose we could find my boots?" asked Viola.

THE END

Acknowledgements

Thank you to Sue Rehorek and the steampunk community, who encouraged me to write more Viola Stewart adventures. A special thank you to the members of my writing group, to my beta readers, and to Sharon Kemmett and David Carlisle who read this through... so many times. Thank you to Katrina Hunt for assisting with Coptic translation and to Terry Brown, of Dragonsblood Creations, who supplied the beautiful gowns worn by the cover model, Zena Alliu.

About the Author

Karen J Carlisle lives in Adelaide with her family and the ghost of her ancient Devon Rex cat. She loves fantasy fiction, gardening, historical re-creation, and steampunk and can often be found plotting fantastical, piratic or airship adventures.
Karen has always loved chocolate and rarely refuses a cup of tea. She is not keen on South Australian summers.

www.karenjcarlisle.com
https://www.patreon.com/KarenJCarlisle
https://ko-fi.com/karenjcarlisle

Follow me at:
www.goodreads.com/KarenJCarlisle
https://www.instagram.com/karenjcarlisle/
https://www.tiktok.com/@karenjcarlisle
https://twitter.com/kjcarlisle

Other works by Karen J Carlisle

The Adventures of Viola Stewart series:
Available in paperback:
Doctor Jack & Other Tales: Journal #1
Eye of the Beholder & Other Tales: Journal #2
The Illusioneer & Other Tales: Journal #3
Also available as eBooks

Other books by Karen J Carlisle:
The Aunt Enid Mysteries
Aunt Enid: Protector Extraordinaire
A Fey Tale

The Department of Curiosities
The Department of Curiosities
Coming soon:
Against the Empire

Also available as eBooks:
Short Story Collections
With a Twist of the Nib: For when time is short
Another Twist of the Nib: Shorter Tales with a Darker Twist
Quarantine Reads: Escape to Adventure

Mrs Hudson Investigates
Mrs Hudson Investigates
The Case of the Forgotten Letter

Bonus Short Story

JOURNAL DE LA LUMIèRE

Access to electrical technology is rare and dangerous. Research is illegal throughout The Empire and most of Europe...
But why?

This short is part of a planned future series, set in a shadowy part of Viola's world, which most never see:

THE WIZARD OF ST GILES
⊕

IOURNAL DE LA LUMIèRE

Rain pattered on the closed shutters. Fingers of light clawed through the slats, piercing the gloom of the townhouse. Muffled hooves clopped along the boulevard. The world moved on.

Inside, all was silent. Ghost-like drop cloths obscured years of memories. Furniture. Keepsakes. Research.

Gone was the endless parade of hopeful students. Gone were the servants. Gone was… Francois.

His sudden demise had changed everything. The Sûreté had given up on the investigation but there were so many unanswered questions.

Elizabeth's footsteps echoed through the foyer, clattered on the steps spiralling down to the dim service passage. She lit an oil lamp, wiped her fingers on her skirt - the soot invisible on the black silk – and shuffled into the darkness.

Keys jangled in her hand as she regarded the locked door. The cellar had been Francois' domain, his personal research laboratory. Only once had she ventured into its depths.

She closed her eyes. His anaemic face still haunted her nightmares, frequented her daydreams.

So pale... A tear crept down her cheek.

Somewhere in the cellar was a box of mementos. Francois had gone to retrieve it on the day he…

Elizabeth fidgeted with the keys. She had tried to ignore it when his research had been entrusted to the university, tried to forget it when his possessions had been packed away, tried to obliterate the memories.

Her brother, Xavier, was arriving this afternoon, to escort her home to England; this was her last chance. What had he been doing?

Elizabeth took a deep breath. The key clicked in the lock. She had to know.

Narrow stone steps led into the cramped cellar. Mountains of crates and jumbled paraphernalia lined the walls. Her eyes glanced over the dark stain on the floor, near the overturned chair, and avoided the deep gouges in the splintered wood of the workbench. She had to find that box.

Elizabeth skirted the cellar edges, examining labels, rummaging through contents until she found a curious tag, attached to a pale crate by a rosary:

To: Father Xavier Andrews,
London, England.

Elizabeth bit her lip.

Xavier? Why would Francois address a box to her brother? She cracked open the crate. A faint odour of rotting flesh clawed at her eyes. She wrinkled her nose and peered into the crate. It smelled like dead rat.

Books filled it to the brim, many untitled. Book after book was retrieved from the depths, flipped through and stacked in a pile beside the box. Most were in Francois' hand.

Elizabeth delved deeper. Her throat tightened. The stench clung to the books. Her fingers brushed against bristles. Her hand flinched, skin crawled. She swallowed and lifted another book, hoping not to find a dead rodent. She had to know.

What was in the box?

Wedged near the bottom of the crate was a rough hessian pouch, tied to a yellow leather-bound journal with a rosary. Elizabeth extracted the pouch from the rosary binding and pulled its strings, to reveal the contents. Dried berries and delicate flowers trickled from the pouch. A wave of nausea drifted over her.

Mayflowers?

Elizabeth retreated, beyond the emanations of the desiccated confetti, and unwound the rosary from the journal. The leather was soft, and smelled of Mayflowers. A portable mirror was inlaid inside the back cover. She turned the pages, her fingers only touching the pages as long as necessary.

It was written in dual hands: one was unfamiliar, seen in an occasional entry or scribbled in a margin. The other was Francois' studious scrawl, with enthusiastic gouges into the paper. Elizabeth smiled, remembering the passionate gleam in her husband's eye as he chased an enigma.

She dabbed her eye and scanned the pages, full of experimental notations and technical diagrams, until she found an entry dated a few months ago:

Nikola has managed to procure the needed equipment. The Sûreté followed him again today. We have now taken precautions to secrete the machine and are in accord. We tell no one of our experiments, not even Elizabeth. It must remain secret. I will not risk her imprisonment for mon décisions téméraires.

Monsieur Nikola Tesla? She remembered a tall man – polite, with fastidiously trimmed moustaches and an incessant drive to work into the early morning hours. He'd worked in the laboratory for months, then a week ago he missed dinner. She had never seen him again.

Elizabeth turned the page. A folded note fluttered to the floor. It was a diagram of the cellar, showing a secret alcove beyond the crates by the far wall. She retrieved the oil lamp and squeezed past the barricade.

A pair of sconces protruded from the blank wall. Elizabeth eyed the crates behind her, and frowned. Surely, any light would be blocked by the barricade.

She re-examined the wall. There should be a door, but there was none. No handle, no seams. She consulted the map. The left sconce had been drawn in a different ink. She yanked on the fixture.

Cogs whirred. Gears clunked. A section of wall detached and slid to one side. Elizabeth peeked inside. A shrouded shadow loomed in the corner of the chamber. Again, the stench invaded her nostrils. She edged the lamp closer. Hawthorn berries and dried Mayflowers wreathed the large canvas-covered intrigue.

Elizabeth held her breath and grabbed the canvas. It slipped to the floor, revealing a contraption - a metal cylinder propped on a mahogany box by four brass columns. Wires protruded from each end of the cylinder, coiling up to two terminals mounted on top of the cylinder. Coils sat between the four columns attached directly to the box. Insulated wires hung loose near three metal switches on the front of the box

Elizabeth gasped.

An Electrical Current Machine! She had heard about them. They were dangerous – and illegal. *What were you up to, Francois?*

She ran her fingertips over the machine, tracing the smooth metal and glass and polished wood of the box-base. A side panel moved under her finger. More papers were wedged inside. Elizabeth examined the diagrams.

Curious. She smiled. No one would know if she just…

The instructions were easy to follow. Elizabeth attached the two wires to the two top box switches, and flipped the naked bottom switch. The contraption hummed. Was it a form of steamless generator?

Elizabeth licked her lips and flipped the left switch. A spark of electricity bridged the gap between the terminals. The hairs on the back of her neck stood up.

Her eyes widened. She consulted the notes, took a deep breath and flipped the remaining switch. Another spark, of brilliant blue, leaped the gap. It crackled and hissed but remained intact. The chamber smelled like the crisp air after a thunderstorm. Elizabeth grinned.

"But what does it do?" she cooed. She snatched up the journal and devoured the words.

Nikola was followed again today. There are more of them now. Paris is no longer safe for him. He has secured passage and will arrive in America on the 6th. We will work separately as long as we are able. Perhaps one of us can find the answer.

A click in the cellar caught Elizabeth's attention. She shivered and glanced over her shoulder. The cellar was dark. She was alone.

Alone... The dark had a way of playing tricks, but not to worry; Xavier would arrive in a few hours.

She returned to the journal: The next entry was less than a week old.

I was attacked by – something fiendish. I have not seen its visage before. The apparatus acted strangely in its presence – flickering and sputtering - as if the creature were consuming the energy. Fortunately, Nikola arrived and fought off the creature. We searched the entire house. It was gone.

Thankfully, Elizabeth was having tea with friends. All was secure before she returned.

Nikola was tardy, as his boat ticket had been stolen. It can't be a coincidence. We have taken precautions- hidden the machine and protected the journal. A box of hawthorne has been ordered.

Another click, and a shuffle. Elizabeth flinched. It was closer this time. She peeked around the edge of the doorway. The cellar was dark. And silent. The contraption's buzz faltered, the blue spark flickered.

The journal fell from Elizabeth's hands. A chill breeze wafted past her cheek. She peered into the darkness.

Nothing

Elizabeth retrieved the journal and wrapped the rosary around her fingers. Another breeze caressed her neck. The lamp flame died. The contraption's eerie glow filled the chamber.

The spark faltered. Elizabeth gripped the pale wooden beads of the rosary and held her breath.

The contraption's hum faded. Its spark fizzled.

A chill drifted into the chamber.

www.ingramcontent.com/pod-product-compliance
Lightning Source LLC
Chambersburg PA
CBHW051923110726
47902CB00002B/396